BLOOD FOR BLOOD

A HARRY BAUER THRILLER

BLAKE BANNER

R

RIGHTHOUSE

PRAISE FOR HARRY BAUER

"Thor, Baldacci, Flynn, Hamburg. Get ready as Banner fits right in!"

AMAZON REVIEW

"Move over Jack Reacher there's a new guy taking over."

AMAZON REVIEW

"Great stuff. Exciting and fast paced. On par with Flynn & Thor."

AMAZON REVIEW

"The writing was superior, the story line was compelling and the action was top-notch. Sorry I could only give this one a five star rating!"

AMAZON REVIEW

ISBN-13: 978-1-63696-328-0

ISBN-10: 1-63696-328-5

Cover design by: Damonza

Printed in the United States of America

www.righthouse.com

www.instagram.com/righthousebooks

www.facebook.com/righthousebooks

twitter.com/righthousebooks

ONE

His throat had been cut from ear to ear. He hadn't been decapitated, but another couple of inches would have done the job. Sheriff Seth Levi asked me, "Is that what they call a Mexican necktie?" Like I was more likely to know than he was. The guy in the white coat who'd let us into the morgue watched me curiously. I shook my head.

"The cut is shorter in a necktie, under the chin, and the tongue is pulled out through the cut. This—" I pointed at the partially blackened wound on the corpse on the metal trolley. "This is more reminiscent of an Islamic execution or retribution." I raised my shoulders half an inch. "But those usually involve a complete decapitation."

The sheriff of Sublette County spent a moment nodding, looking down at his boots and chewing on his lip. When he spoke, his tone was dry. "We don't get a lot of Islamic terrorists up here, Harry. Did you know him? He had your name on a piece of paper in his pocket."

"Yeah." I looked at the face. It was a face I had grown

accustomed to seeing in laughter and defiance. "His name was Ernie. Ernie Skinner. He was from the East End of London, England. We spent eight years together in the SAS. We joined on the same day. I heard he left shortly after I did."

"You didn't stay in touch?"

I gave my head a small shake.

"You fell out over something?"

I gave a smile that was rueful. "No, nothing like that. When you go through Special Ops together, you create a bond that is stronger than brotherhood, Seth. But for some reason, when you leave the service, you don't stay in touch. Most of the memories you share are things you'd rather forget." I glanced at him. "Can I see the paper?"

"It's next door, in my office. There was a bandana, too. You're certain of your identification?"

I gazed at the waxy, lifeless lump of flesh that had once housed the soul of one of my closest friends. "Yeah," I said. "That was Ernie."

"OK. Thanks, Ret." This last was directed at the guy in the white coat who'd led us to the body. Seth turned, and I followed him through the swing doors. "Any idea what this guy Ernie was doing here?"

"Looking for me would seem to be the simple answer."

We'd come to the broad staircase, and I followed him down.

"That much is obvious, Harry."

He didn't speak again until we'd come to the sheriff's department and he'd led me to his office. There he kicked back in his chair behind his desk, laced his fingers across his belly, and watched me sit.

"Harry, I am going to be straight with you. You and me are friends. I respect you, but I know you've got a history, and I do not want any of this shit in my town. I am going to show you some things, and I am going to ask you some questions, and I am going to trust you to be straight with me. My responsibility is to the people of this county. These people are as tough as they come, but they have no experience dealing with special operatives or Islamic terrorists. I need you to come clean."

I drew breath, but he cut me short. "Don't talk till I ask you."

He sat forward and opened a drawer. From it he withdrew a piece of paper in a transparent evidence bag. The sheet was roughly three inches square, and here and there it was crumpled and torn. The handwriting on it might have been his. It said simply, *Harry Bauer - Pinedale, Wyoming*. Below that was Claire's address.

"What you told me, Harry, when you moved up here to be with Claire, was that nobody knew where you'd gone."

"Very few people knew."

"Was he one of them?"

I gave my head a single, slow shake. "No. He wasn't one of them."

"I need to know how he found out, why he was looking for you, and who cut his throat."

"You and me both, Seth."

"Right." He didn't sound thrilled by the prospect. He reached in the drawer again and pulled out a bandana in a larger, plastic evidence bag. He tossed it on the desk in front of me. Embroidered into the cloth was the word *Intiquaam*.

I didn't touch it. He watched me looking at it for a moment. Finally he asked me, "What does it mean?"

"You haven't googled it?"

"I want you to tell me."

"It means revenge."

"In what language, Harry?"

I shifted my eyes up, to take in his face. "In Arabic," I said. "It means revenge in Arabic."

He held my eye for a moment. "I don't want this shit in my county. But I don't need to tell you, Harry, that in order to deal with a problem, you need to know first what that problem is. So what's this about?"

I went to speak several times, but my jaw had other ideas and bit back on the words.

"Harry?"

"I don't know."

He stood and went and filled a couple of mugs with the black water he called coffee. While they were filling, he was looking out the window at the trees on South Tyler Avenue. He spoke suddenly, as if half in a dream.

"The State issued a questionnaire." He blinked and turned to look at me. "Did they want wolves reintroduced into the area? They were Canadian wolves. They said there would be ecological advantages, but the people knew better and said no. They didn't want wolves because they'd be a danger to livestock."

He took the mugs and handed me one. Then he sat.

"They introduced them anyway. A couple of months back, a young man on his snowmobile saw one of the wolves. He ran it over, taped up its mouth, tortured it, and dragged it over to a bar in Daniel, where he exhibited it before taking it out to the parking lot and shooting it."

"Son of a bitch."

"He and his family had to leave the county because of death threats."

"Why are you telling me this, Seth?"

"We are tough people, Harry. Struggling and overcoming is built into our DNA. Sometimes, especially among the younger men, they have a pretty uncompromising way of dealing with things. Now I'm figuring a couple of Iranian hit men might stand out in Pinedale, and if you bring a war of retribution with some Islamic hit squad to this county, some of these patriotic boys might decide to get involved, and they could end up biting off more than they know."

I shook my head. "That won't happen. I'll leave. They'll come after me."

"Are you sure?" I frowned at him. He arched an eyebrow. "Are you leaving anything behind? Anything they could use against you?"

I sagged into my chair. "I promised her I would never come back here."

"Yeah, well." He sat forward and placed his elbows on the desk with his fists cupped in front of him. "Walking away ain't always the best solution," he said ambiguously. "You need to brief me on this, Harry. I need to know what I am looking at."

I spent a long time staring at my cup. I wasn't seeing it. I was seeing Ernie, standing by the Jeep in the sand, in the bright glare of the sun.

"Afghans," I said. "Not Iranians. We were carrying out regular patrols in the Helmand Province. Mainly it was intelligence gathering, though occasionally we would use that 'intel' to call in a strike. More rarely, we would perform sabotage operations or hit camps."

I sipped the coffee. It was as bad as I thought it would be.

"Most of the villages down there are tiny. Some are just hamlets in the sand with maybe five families sharing the work of caring for goats and cultivating what little can be grown on the banks of the Helmand River. The vast majority of them are Muslims with the kind of commitment to religion you get from people with more pressing problems to worry about, like eating and surviving day to day."

"What does that mean?"

"It means that over a short period of time, some of these villagers came to realize they had more to fear from the Taliban than from us. In addition, in some of these villages, as well as Muslims, the population was a mix of Christians, Sikhs, and even Hindus. They kept quiet about it, but we came to know which ones they were because in time they began to leave out food and water for us."

He was frowning. "No kidding."

"There was one village in particular. It was called Al-Landy. We never went in—that would have been too dangerous for us and even more so for them—but we'd gotten to the point of leaving coded messages for each other. I mean basic stuff like 'thanks' 'be careful' 'God is with you.' The most sophisticated one we received was 'Patrol to the north this week.' Needless to say, that patrol didn't last the week. But during the time we were patrolling the desert around that village, Ernie spotted a girl among the townsfolk. She must have been in her teens, just a few years younger than him. She was pretty and seemed spirited and fun. They never met or talked, but he used to watch her through his scope and his binoculars, and she must have spied on him when we collected the gifts they left for us. He used to say that when the war was over, he'd come back for her."

I went quiet. For a long while, I couldn't make the words come. Eventually I took a deep breath and puffed out my cheeks.

"Somehow a local chieftain called Mohammed Ben-Amini got wind that this village was not doing its share for global jihad, and he and his two nephews, Del and Gabbai, drove in with maybe a hundred men in their Toyota pickups and their Jeeps. They rounded up those dangerous women, children, and old farmers, and they raped them and tortured them and murdered them until there was not one left alive. We were in the hills outside the village. It scarred us all for life. A couple of us wanted to go in, but the guy in charge stopped us. The four of us would have been killed, and we knew the more damage we did to them before they killed us the more suffering would be inflicted on the villagers. So we had to stand by and let it happen.

"Not one of us came away unscarred, but Ernie and I wanted revenge. We talked about it, and we roped in two other guys who had seen similar things. There was me and Ernie, Dave and Sergeant Bradley, the Kiwi. We got drunk in a bar in Kabul, and we decided to go for it."

"Go for what, Harry?"

"Revenge." I drained my cup and shifted in my seat. "We work in teams of four. We call them patrols. So the four of us would all volunteer for the same patrols. Everybody knew what we were doing, and nobody gave a rat's ass. On the contrary. They all supported us. Provided we kept it slick and professional and it didn't get in the way of our designated missions, it just helped the war effort. So we went after any Taliban gang in the area, but especially we hunted down Mohammed Ben-Amini's little army.

"We learned eventually that they had mustered a large posse—maybe two hundred men—to hunt us down, and they were camped nearby. We all got a bit crazy one afternoon, grabbed two Jeeps with mounted M134 miniguns in back, and headed for their camp.

"We reached it at nightfall, bid each other farewell, because there was no way we were coming out alive, and we plowed into the camp with the guns blazing. We took out the guards, stunned where they stood, and just stormed right into the encampment. There were just two Jeeps. Each had one guy on the minigun, and the driver driving like a madman, steering with one hand and firing RPGs with the other." I gave a small laugh. "Though I say so myself, it was a master class in the use of surprise. We drove right into the center of the camp, pouring lead into the tents. Every ten or fifteen seconds, one of us would fire an RPG.

"I think out of two hundred plus men, maybe twenty or thirty made it out of the tents, and they were gunned down as they emerged. We massacred them as they fought to scramble out of the collapsing canvas. After less than five minutes, it was over. It was Ernie who had the idea. He went and took one of their keffiyeh scarves from around the dead guy's head, and in his blood he wrote *Intiquaam* and suspended it from one of the few tent poles left standing. Intiquaam, revenge for the lover he never had."

I paused and drank the last few dregs from my cup, then set it on his desk and leaned forward.

"Shortly after that, we found and captured Mohammed Ben-Amini. A captain in the CIA took him into custody but accused me of being about to execute him without trial.[1] As a result, I was asked to resign from the SAS, rather than being kicked out."

The sheriff raised an eyebrow at me. "Naturally, the charge was completely false."

I shook my head. "Nope. It was absolutely correct."

He nodded for a while, blinking at me. "Right. So who killed your friend Ernie?"

"I honestly don't know. But I can point to the stinking cesspit they came from."

He sighed heavily. "That's quite a story. I'll be honest with you, Harry. I don't have the resources to deal with this kind of situation. And more to the point, I don't want Sublette County to be the kind of place that has those resources. What are you going to do?"

"My money is on this being a squad of jihadists bent on revenge, and I can hazard a guess who's leading it. So I'm going to find out who is in the squad, I am going to lead them away from Pinedale, and I am going to kill them. All."

He closed his eyes. "Sweet Jesus."

I shook my head. "This ain't his fight. He has other things to worry about. Leave this one to me."

He didn't look happy. "There is something else you need to know."

"What?"

---

1. See *Dead of Night*

"Your friend Ernie found his way to Claire's house before he disappeared and turned up dead. She told me he gave her a message that she could only pass on to you." I sighed, but before I could say anything, he went on. "She's willing to see you, Harry, for a short visit, and I should tell you she's with a new man. Don't cause trouble."

I nodded. "Thanks."

I stood and left.

TWO

I ROLLED DOWN THE BROAD CURVE OF THE HILL that led from the Clinic and the Mountain Man Museum to the sprawl of Pinedale itself. Muscle memory carried me along Pine Street as far as Stockman's restaurant, where I turned into Maybell Avenue with a hot twist in my gut.

Her house—the house that had almost been ours—stood on the corner of Magnolia Street. It was a traditional two-story cabin made of logs, set behind broad lawns shaded by enough giant pine trees to make a small woodland. I swung down from the cab of my Jeep, and when I looked at the white door at the end of the path, for a moment I felt sick.

She opened the door almost immediately and stood staring at me, holding the door like it was a defensive shield. She didn't say anything. So I took a deep breath and said, "Hi."

She stepped back. "You'd better come in."

I stepped over the threshold. She closed the door and

brushed past me, moving quickly to the kitchen. The kitchen where we had so often had breakfast together, where I was now an unwelcome outsider.

She stood at the sink with her back to me and spoke without turning around.

"I told you I didn't want any of this. After Burunda, you told me you'd make sure nothing like this would ever happen again. You promised.[1]"

"Yeah, I also told you not to go to Burunda. But it seems some things stick in the memory better than others."

She turned to stare at me, and her eyes were angry. "You *promised!*"

I fought to hold my own anger back.

"Yeah, Claire, but there are some things I can't control. Along with all the other things you've forgotten, you seem to have forgotten that I am only a human being. I can't control the decisions taken by drug barons and terrorist warlords." Before she could answer, I added, "And please don't remind me again that I promised. I am here to make good on that promise as best I can. At least I make that effort to see it through. Others just walk away when the going gets tough."

Her voice was barely a whisper. "That isn't fair."

"No, life isn't. So if you're done pointing your finger and distributing blame, maybe you can answer me a couple of questions and I can get out of your life and leave you in peace. With some luck, you'll never see me again."

She closed her eyes. "I didn't mean..." She reached for a chair at the kitchen table and sat. I said, with more bitterness

---

1. See *The Devil's Vengeance*

than I intended, "Can I sit down, or is this an interview I have to do standing up?"

"Please stop, Harry. Sit down."

I pulled out the chair and sat. "I came here intending to be civil and make this as painless as possible. But practically the first thing you say to me when I was through the door is an accusation. Like this was my fault. So don't tell me to stop."

Her eyes were closed again. "Are you done?"

"I hope so. Are you?"

She gave a single nod. Her eyes were still closed. I spoke more quietly.

"I just came from the morgue. The dead man was one of my closest friends. We joined the Regiment together. We were in Afghanistan together. His name was Ernie. He was more than a brother."

"I'm sorry."

"Seth said he came here to talk to you. Did you let him in?"

"Of course, Harry. I'm not—"

"Did you talk?"

She sighed quietly. "We talked for a short while. He said he was looking for you. He wanted to know if I knew where you were. I told him I didn't know. I told him to talk to Seth. I guessed Seth would know how to contact you."

"Yeah, he contacted me when Ernie was already dead. Did he say anything else? You said you were talking for a while."

She took a deep breath and gave her head a small shake. "Do you want some coffee?"

"I don't want to cause inconvenience—"

"Stop it, Harry. This is difficult for both of us. Do you want a coffee?"

"Yes."

She stood with her back to me again, reaching for cups, filling the glass jug.

"He said it was important." She stopped, leaning on the side with both hands, looking down. "Harry, I'm sorry. I didn't really listen. I just wanted him to go away. Every minute he was here, I was back in Burunda..."

She trailed off. There was a moment of silence. The coffee started to gurgle, spit, and hiss. I wanted to tell her it was OK, she couldn't have known how serious it was, she wasn't responsible. But every word felt like a lie.

She brought the jug and two cups to the table and poured.

"He said—" She handed me a cup. "He said an old friend had been in touch."

I frowned. "An old friend?"

"Yes, I'm afraid he didn't seem to make a lot of sense, and I—"

"Did he mention a name or anything about this friend?"

Her gaze shifted over to the window. A cloud moved imperceptibly, high in the blue. A tree bowed gently but made no sound. She said, "Yes" but kept staring at the glass. "He said it was your old friend Ben." She frowned. "Then said something. That Cockney accent was hard to follow sometimes. He said it wasn't Ben really because Ben—because Ben had"—she hesitated—"kicked the bucket?" I nodded. "But it was Ben's cousins. Uh... Del and Gabby? Can that be right?"

"Yeah, that's right. Did he say where he had seen them?"

"He said he'd seen them in New York, but he'd heard from"—she hesitated again—"the Kiwi?"

"Yeah."

"He'd heard from the Kiwi that you'd moved to Pinedale, and he came to tell you. I'm sorry. It doesn't make much sense, but really I just wanted him to leave, so I wasn't really listening. And now he's dead. Some doctor, huh?"

I didn't look at her. I looked into the black coffee in my cup. "You're not responsible for Ernie's death. Whoever cut his throat is responsible." After a moment, I added, "You were just trying to protect your home and your family."

She flashed a look at me. "Harry—"

I shook my head. "If you think of anything else, tell Seth. He'll send it on. I'm leaving now. If these guys are still here looking for me, I'll lead them away. Thanks for the coffee."

"Harry—"

"Don't. Let it go. Be happy. I'll see myself out."

She didn't follow me out or come running after me and fling herself into my arms as I tried to board the Jeep. That only happens in the movies. I closed the door behind me, and it stayed closed. I climbed into my Jeep and drove away, not knowing exactly where I was going, only that I had to go. I turned left and east onto Pinedale Road and followed it out of town toward Boulder, but at the intersection, I took Pole Creek Road, and two and a half miles in, at the bend before the hill, I slowed and pulled off at the mailbox beside the gate.

There I climbed out and leaned on the heavy wooden bar. It was padlocked. It was up for sale, theoretically at least.

I had bought it for 'us.' But it turned out in the end there had never been an 'us' to buy it for. It had just been me, and the place was still mine. Up on the hill, maybe half a mile away, hidden among aspen trees and pines, I could see the big house, constructed of heavy, dark logs. The gabled roof with the tall stone chimney and down below, the decking that went all around the house. I smiled to myself. In Wyoming, you don't have a porch or patio. In the Cowboy State, you have decking. That's where you sit, drink beer, and shoot the breeze.

On an impulse, I vaulted the fence and walked the half mile to the big cabin. It was all locked up. I'd brought the keys in case I needed to stay, but now that I was here, I didn't want to open the door or go inside. There were too many ghosts in there, and I didn't want to let them out.

Instead I walked around till I came to the east deck, and there I sat on the boards, looking out across the sagebrush toward the jagged, towering peaks of the Wind River Mountains—the Winds.

He had never come here to see this place as a friend. We had never sat out on the deck and drunk whiskey and talked. He had come here to die—to warn me and to die.

A movement made me look. Down below, a moose and her yearlings stood by the stream chewing at the willows where they sprang from the wet soil. I smiled to myself.

"Fearlessness is better than a faint heart," I recited quietly to myself, "for any man who would poke his nose out of doors. The length of my life and the day of my death were fated long ago."

Ernie had never feared death. None of us had. When it

came, it came. Until then, you lived as best you could —fearlessly.

I pulled out my phone, found the brigadier, and dialed his number.

"Harry, this is a pleasant surprise. Where are you?"

"I'm in Pinedale, Wyoming."

He was quiet for so long I thought he'd moved away from the phone. Eventually he just said, "Oh, I see. Something you want to tell me about?"

"The sheriff called me in the small hours of last night. Said he needed me here ASAP. I got an air taxi and arrived this morning."

"Is Claire all right?"

"Yeah. She's fine. It was Ernie."

"Ernie Skinner?"

"He had a piece of paper in his pocket with my name on it and Claire's address. He'd been asking around for me. They found him out by Freemont Lake with his throat cut ear to ear and a knife stuck in his back with a *keffiyeh* hanging from it. There was writing on it. It said *Intiquaam*."

I paused. I heard him grunt. I went on.

"He spoke to Claire shortly before he died. He told her Ben was dead, but his cousins Del and Gabbai were looking for me."

"Del and Gabbai, Mohammed Ben-Amini's nephews, his right-hand men. There were rumors they had created some kind of revenge sect."

"Yeah, well it looks like the rumors weren't rumors after all. The smart money says that sect is called Intiquaam, revenge, and they are out to punish Ernie's gang of four."

He was quiet for a while, then asked the obvious question. "Why now? It must be years."

"Maybe they only just got out of the hospital." I let the smile show in my voice and heard him chuckle.

"What do you need from me? You know anything from the Regiment will have to be unofficial."

"I just need to know where Dave and the Kiwi are."

"I'll have to check on Sergeant Bradley, but David Gaunt is in Hollywood."

I scowled. "Hollywood? What the hell is he doing, private security to the stars?"

"No, my dear chap, he is shooting a series. One SAS man confronting a whole array of ninjas and martial arts experts in a whole variety of settings."

I shook my head and sighed. "Yup, that's Dave. You have an address for him?"

"I'll send it to you. But Harry, with the high profile he has at the moment, I wouldn't phone him. They might be monitoring his calls. Maybe contact his agent, Saul Bernstein."

"Sure. I won't let him know I'm coming. Thank you, sir."

"Take care. Keep me posted and let me know if you need anything."

I hung up and paused a while, watching the moose and her kids. I thought of all the people who would want to kill them just because they were beautiful. Finally I checked my messages. There was one from the brigadier. It had Dave's address and phone with the repeated advice not to contact him unless it was essential.

A second message had Saul Bernstein's telephone number and the address of his office on Sunset Boulevard.

I called a couple of times, and it went to voicemail. So I made my way back to the Jeep and headed for Jackson Hole Airport without having unpacked my bags.

THREE

SAUL BERNSTEIN WAS IN GOOD FORM. HE WAS SIX foot six, bony, and moved to the music like an articulated aspen in a high wind, jostling the people beside him. The music was too loud, so people had to shout to be heard, but the general consensus was that they had nothing worth saying anyway, so they laughed instead. Over the laughter and the thumping music, there was a scream followed by a splash.

Saul progressed through the crowd with his eyes closed, moving his long arms and legs. He was thinking about his wife who had divorced him after twenty years. She'd kept the house and the mortgage, but he'd kept the clients and the parties.

"Ha!"

He approached the bar as though by radar and opened his eyes. There was a young, dark-skinned man behind the white linen and the bottles.

"Mejicano?" asked Saul facetiously and probably a little offensively.

"No, sir, American. What can I get you?"

Saul pointed at him. "I need three things, a pretty woman to give me a little *leeeervin!* A couple of ounces of devil's dandruff, you know what I am saying, amigo?"

The boy smiled and gave a small shrug. "Mr. D won't allow us to do that, Mr. Bernstein." He leaned forward and spoke quietly. "But word is there is a room inside—they call it the Hall of Mirrors, and I am sure I don't need to tell you why." He straightened up. "So what is the third thing on your list?"

"A glass of cold, cold champagne." But Saul was frowning, and the bounce had gone out of his step. "Hall of mirrors, huh? So me and Matt go back a long way. How come he never told me about this room?"

The boy poured him a glass of Dom Perignon and gave a small laugh. "That's simple, Mr. Bernstein. The room is not reserved for extra exclusive guests; otherwise you'd have known about it for sure."

"Right?"

"Mr. D's rule is, 'If they are looking for that, let them ask me.' Because he himself does not indulge."

"Huh, right..."

"And you yourself are generally socializing, mixing—a people person. Usually you are not..." He sniffed and ran his finger back and forth across his nose.

"Right." Saul lifted his chin and gave a few nods. "You're a smart kid. What are you looking for in life? You a singer, dancer, actor...?"

"Aaah, no, Mr. Bernstein. I am just here to bring a little joy into people's lives."

"No kidding?"

"You want me to find that room for you?"

"You'd do that?"

"Of course I would, Mr. Bernstein. Don't stray far. I'll be right back."

The boy left, and Saul turned to look at the milling crowd and the people who were beginning to strip off and leap into the pool. The girls, all with perfect bodies, were screaming. Thee guys were laughing. He noticed a few of the girls strip off their tops, smiled to himself, and decided to move in for a closer look. If any of them was a client of his, he might talk to her about a movie a close friend of his was producing...

He draped a lecherous leer on his lips and moved across the lawn. He scanned the flesh splashing in the illuminated pool. He recognized there a girl he represented. He had gotten her the invite to the party. May? Day? May Day? Darryl May. That was it. And there was no question she was a damned sight better with her clothes off than on.

He felt the gentle tap on his shoulder. He turned to see the young waiter behind him.

"Mr. Bernstein, would you like to follow me?"

Saul grinned. "I sure would."

They crossed the lawn and climbed the steps to the broad terrace where the sliding glass doors stood open onto the glittering drawing room. The boy led the way through the glittering crowd, and Saul mused drunkenly that if it had been a movie and this were the glittering cast, you'd need the budget of a small European country just to pay the actors.

As he passed, Jack offered him a lupine leer from behind his bowtie. Saul leered back. Kate pretended to ignore him but then winked. She knew he could still make things happen for her, now that she was approaching the big five-oh. Leo, now on his way to becoming one of the venerable old men of Hollywood, slapped him on the shoulder as he began to climb the staircase to the upper floor, following the anonymous waiter.

The anonymous waiter—The Anonymous Waiter—not a bad title for a movie. A dark thriller, perhaps, with a hint of the supernatural. Tag line: Here to Bring a Little Joy...nah. He is Here to Serve. Nah, crap. Be Careful What You Order...

They were moving down the red carpet on the landing. The banisters and the walls were white. The waiter disappeared around a dogleg, past a fat urn with a palm in it. Saul rounded the same corner and saw, maybe fifteen feet ahead of him, a door standing open. The waiter's head emerged and smiled.

"In here, Mr. Bernstein."

Saul grinned and stepped through the door. The waiter closed it behind him. It was a small sitting room, part of a suite. The bedroom was through a door to the right. At the far end of the room, sage green drapes were closed across the window. There was a small roll top desk and a captain's chair. Immediately in front of him there was a sofa and a couple of chairs gathered around a glass coffee table. On the table there was an exotic-looking silver box which stood open with a teaspoon beside it. Beside the spoon, there was a square mirror.

Saul grinned and made a move toward the sofa. The young waiter said, "Sir...?"

Saul stared at him a moment, then laughed. "Oh! Right!"

He reached in his pocket and pulled out his wallet. From there, he took twenty bucks and handed it to the boy. They boy looked at it a moment and shook his head.

"Oh, I can't take that, Mr. Bernstein."

Saul frowned. "Why not?" Then he laughed. "You want a snort instead?" He stuffed the twenty in the boy's jacket and went and sat. As he spread the powder on the mirror, the waiter said, "I couldn't do that either, sir. It's against my religion."

Saul scraped out a line. "Yeah? What's your religion?" He took the straw from the silver box and snorted hard. His mouth sagged open. He closed his eyes and fell back on the sofa, laughing. He whooped, opened his eyes, and grinned at the boy. The grin froze, then faded from his face.

"I am a Muslim." He was holding a suppressed Glock in his hands. "Take your pen and a piece of paper, and you write down for me David Gaunt's address and his private telephone number. Also the current location of filming."

"What the fuck...?"

"That is the first and last time you stall. Next time I put a bullet in your right knee. Do it now."

He fumbled. Hot terror twisted his gut, and his hands shook so badly he could hardly get a hold of his pen. He dropped it on the table, spilling white powder, and held up both hands, "Wait! Wait, I'm...just take it easy."

The waiter stepped forward and dropped a small pad on the table.

"Write."

The coke mixed with the adrenaline and made his hands tremble so hard he couldn't hold the pen. "Just, just give me a second. I can, I can do this. Just give me…"

"Write."

Somehow he managed to scrawl the address and Dave's phone number on the pad. Then a wet, pathetic grin creased his face, and his laugh came high-pitched and shrill. "You know, you only had to ask! I would have…"

Something in the young waiter's eyes made him trail off. He knew death was in those eyes. His own death. The young man reached out, pointing at him with the fat, bloated suppressor. The last word he heard before it spat molten flames was, "Jew!"

———

THE DESERT SUN burned into his eyes, nagged at the headache at the back of his neck, and drew his stomach menacingly toward his mouth. He knew he wouldn't vomit. He had nothing left to vomit. But that didn't make him feel any less sick.

He pushed on his black Wayfarers and peered at the scene where the action was being shot. His instinct was to tell them all to go to hell and go home to sleep it off until the next day at the least. Who the hell throws a party full of expensive booze and eighteen-year-old babes the day before you start shooting?

And where the fuck was Saul when he needed him? If Saul was here, he'd tell him to make his excuses and drive him home. He hadn't had a hangover like this since he was, well, eighteen.

He reached in his jacket pocket and pulled out his cell. Thirty yards away, the director was working with the ninja, talking, positioning. The ninja was doing his ballet moves, and that made Dave snigger as he identified the six ways he would have killed him before his foot touched the ground. He dialed Saul and put the phone to his ear. It rang a dozen times, then went to voicemail. He left a message.

"Saul, you pisshead! What were you thinking, man? You take me to a party, get me drunk, get me laid by not two, but three girls who want to be on the show, and then you let me turn up here alone to play James Bond! You need to come and get me, mate. Make my excuses, protect me, and get me to my home where I can recover. No more bloody parties, Saul!"

He hung up and groaned as he saw the director dispatch a gofer to come and get him. The gofer came running through the heat and the dust, shouting, "Mr. Gaunt! Mr. Gaunt to the set! Mr. Gaunt!"

He stood and groaned again, more loudly, waved listlessly at the boy, and made his way to the set, which was really no more than a patch of desert with views of the mountains in the distance. The director, Paul Grenache, grinned at him as he approached.

"Dave, ready for the fight?" He bent his legs slightly and made some ineffectual punches. He was short, dressed in khaki, and had an accent nobody could identify.

Dave shook his head. "No. I want to go home."

Paul turned "Ooooh-kay," into a laugh, put his hand on Dave's shoulder, and led him to the spot in the dust where the ninja was standing, waiting. He was saying, "So I been talking with the choreographer, and she gonna come in a while and go over this with you, but right now, what we lookin' at is how the camera gonna see you. OK?"

"Right."

"So you gonna be standing here, on this spot, looking out that way, chin up, you gotta handsome, noble face, we wanna see that, squinting slightly. You know danger is out there, watching you, you ready for it! Right?"

Dave nodded. "Danger is out there, that's why I am standing here in the middle of the desert where everyone can see me and shoot me."

"Right, ooooh-kay! So then, Lee is gonna just kind of, *wham! Be* there! And you gonna be like, '*Wha? What the —?*' And he's gonna go, one, two three!"

This last was accompanied by three blows: one to the face, one to the floating rib, and a chop to the side of the neck.

"And you just kind of stunned, stagger back. This is a fuckin' ninja right? Out of *nowhere!*" He gestured to Lee the Ninja. "You demonstrate." To Dave, he said, "You just standin' there, lookin', listening, *smellin'*... Go!"

David stood gazing at the horizon, trying to ignore the voice in his head that told him this was stupid. Lee the Ninja leapt into the shot with a flapping of black cloth and a flurry of hand movements telegraphed well ahead that the punch was coming.

Instinctively Dave weaved to the side, trapped the wrist, kicked Lee's feet from under him, and took the ninja's blade from his sash belt as he went down. By the time Lee hit the ground, Dave was kneeling on his chest with the blade to his throat. He looked up at Paul and smiled. "Like that?"

"I can't work like this. How can I—? I can't! I can't work like this!"

Dave watched him walk away toward the trailers. He smiled down at the ninja. "All right, mate?"

"That really hurt."

"Be one with the pain, mate. Always works for me."

He stood and followed Grenache toward the trailers. On the way, he pulled his phone from his pocket and called Saul again. It rang and rang, but there was no reply.

FOUR

I had a Grand Cherokee waiting for me at LAX. I-405 got me to Santa Monica Boulevard, and Dave's place was just four miles up the road on North Doheny Drive. Ten minutes later, I pulled up outside a sprawling bungalow that wasn't really big enough to sprawl but did its best. It had banana trees growing out front, redbrick steps up to an big, oak front door that would have been more at home in a medieval castle, and a bare stone chimney poking out of the middle of a pyramidal tiled roof which rose at the center of the sprawl. It was a bungalow that wanted badly to be in Beverly Hills but was stuck in West Hollywood.

I sat for a minute at the wheel, watching the house. There was no activity. From what I could make out through the bow window, the drapes were open, but I could see no movement. Finally I climbed out and walked down the path to the door. I rang the bell, then hammered. That was when I noticed that the door was open because it swung in a few inches.

I stood and listened. I couldn't hear movement; no splashes from the pool, not even the rustle of pages from a book or a magazine. I eased the door open and stepped through, and as I closed it behind me, I slipped the Sig from under my arm.

I was in a big, open plan room made up of different spaces on different levels. What would have been the living room was a circular pit. There was a redbrick fireplace in the middle that looked more like a free-standing barbeque with a beaten bronze hood suspended six feet above it. I approached and felt it. It was clean and cool.

Over on the left, three long, highly polished wooden steps rose to a dining area with access, through sliding glass panels, to the yard and the pool. A glance showed me there was nobody out there, and nowhere to hide, unless they were underwater in the pool.

Between the dining area and the entrance, there was a short passage down to the left. It was dark, and I moved in slowly as far as the first door on my right. I inched it open, and it proved to be a large, marble bathroom with a green marble bath, a shower cubicle, and a strong smell of expensive aftershave.

The next door on the left was a second bedroom that was in the process of being converted into a den, with bookcases, an oak desk, and boxes of books scattered at random around the floor.

I found Dave beyond the last door, in the master bedroom. The bed was unmade. Black and red satin sheets were strewn on the floor. The sliding doors to the pool stood open, and he lay on the floor just inside, face down.

For a few seconds, I felt a violent distress in my head.

Ernie, now Dave, both killed by the living shadows of their past. A past I had shared with them, from which I had not been able to protect them.

I stepped over the rumpled sheets, hunkered down, and took his wrist. I got one beat from his pulse before I had a Sig 320 shoved in my face. His face was still buried in black satin, and his voice sounded like it smelt of last night's stale booze.

"You have three seconds to let go of my wrist. One—"

I let go of his wrist, and it flopped on the floor like he was dead, but the 320 was still eyeballing me.

"Dave, it's Harry."

"Harry?" He said it into the sheets and lifted his face half an inch. "Harry." He narrowed puffy eyes at the bed. "Harry the Wanky Yankee?"

I stood. "Put your damned gun away, go throw up, and have a shower. Have you got any food in this place?"

"Hang on, you little toad." He staggered to his feet, and I was relieved to see he had his shorts on, because the next thing he did was to grab me in a bear hug, slapping me on the back and saying, "What the fuck? Where did you come from? How the bloody hell—?"

He held me at arm's length and grinned at me. I returned the hug with feeling, then slapped him on the shoulder and said, "Instructions as before."

He shuffled toward the bathroom, saying, "Yeah, man, eggs and bacon in the fridge, and good English bangers, mushrooms..."

Whatever came next was drowned out by the shower.

The only cure I know for a hangover, that actually works, is lots of fried protein: bacon, eggs, pork sausages, and some toast and mushrooms thrown in just for decoration. You sit and look at it and you wish you'd been shot during the night, but once you manage to swallow the first bite, you start to feel better.

Dave showed up after five minutes with bare feet, jeans, and a sweatshirt. He frowned at me like he couldn't work out whether he was still dreaming and set to on the plate I'd put before him, pausing only occasionally to drain his cup of black coffee and refill it.

I waited till he'd finished and sat back in his chair. Then he squinted hard at me and said, "What the bloody hell are you doing here?"

"It's good to see you too, Dave."

"No." He shrugged and spread his hands, "Pff! Great to see you, mate. You know that. But what the hell are you doing here?"

"Looking for you."

"Yeah, well, I got that far after the first piece of bacon. But I mean, what is it? You miss my pretty blue eyes, the way I belch when I get up in the morning...?" He shook his head for a bit, then shrugged. "What are you doing here, Harry?"

"Ernie's dead."

Nothing changed on his face. "I'm sorry to hear that. I liked Ernie. He was a good'un." Suddenly he grinned. "We stirred up some shit, ay? You and me and Ernie, and that miserable bastard Bradley, the Kiwi."

I smiled and nodded. "We did."

He was still grinning. "Anyone ever tell you what we called you out there?"

"I know you're about to."

His face creased up, and he started to laugh. "We called you Boomer."

"Boomer?"

"Yeah. Somebody would say to you, 'Hey, Harry, go and take out the guard at the top of that hill. Make it silent.' Anyone else would get out the old Fairbairn-Sykes and cut the bugger's throat." He started to laugh again. "But not our Harry. Harry goes and shoves a grenade up his arse and says, 'His guts muffled the explosion, mate!'"

He laughed so hard I thought he was going to fall off his chair. I laughed too.

"You use what you have to hand, right?"

"Right, mate." The laughter faded from his face, and he sighed. "So, not that it ain't great to see you. It is. But you couldn't have dropped me a line in the post? Where are you? I heard you was in New York. They've got post boxes there."

"I'm in New York some of the time. I had a place in Wyoming."

"Nice."

"Ernie was killed in Wyoming."

"Killed..."

I nodded. "He had his throat cut, ear to ear. He was looking for me at the time. He'd obviously heard I'd moved out there but didn't know I'd moved back."

"Who killed him? That cut..."

"They left a calling card: a head scarf with the word Intiquaam embroidered on it."

"Revenge."

"Yeah, and apparently he was talking about 'Del and Gabby.'"

"Mohammed Ben-Amini's right-hand men, his nephews, Del and Gabbai."

I nodded. "They want their eye for an eye."

He stared at his plate for a moment, then shifted his gaze to me and frowned.

"They'll fuckin get it, mate."

"I spoke to the brigadier."

"Buddy Bird?"

"Yeah. He said the Regiment can't get involved, but unofficially, anything we need."

"Nice. We was breaking the rules when we went after Ben-Amini. But Ernie was hurting bad. We all were."

"I need to find the Kiwi, and we need to make a plan. The plan is find Del and Gabbai, kill them and whoever is working with them, and finish what we started out in Helmand."

"Yeah." He peered in his mug, then refilled it with black coffee. "And try not to lose this contract in the process. It's half a million bucks per episode."

"OK, and try not to lose your job in the process." I sat forward. "Now this is important. Ernie was not an easy man to catch by surprise. Add to that the fact that he knew we were under threat—that's why he was looking for me. Even so, they caught him and cut his throat, and there was no sign of a struggle." I pointed at him. "You have a high profile. You are easy to find and easy to watch. So you want to cut the party lifestyle and get on red alert. When I got here this morning, you had front and back doors open and you were unconscious. If I had been Del or Gabbai, or one of their men, you'd be dead right now."

He grunted. "What about the Kiwi?"

"I'm waiting on the brigadier to tell me where he is. As soon as I know, I'll go get him."

"Bring him here?"

We stared at each other for a long moment, thinking almost telepathically. He glanced at the clock on the wall.

"I need to be on set. Come with me. You'll have my back. I'll have yours. And you can see some of these bloody clowns they have me up against."

I nodded but didn't say anything. He grabbed his things, and we headed out for the car.

We took Santa Monica Boulevard south as far as West LA and Japantown, then made a big U and followed I-10 out toward Redlands and Beaumont. As we passed Ontario, I asked him, "Where are you shooting?"

"Salton Sea? You know it?"

"I know it," I said and gazed out the window at the endless ugliness of Los Angeles' concrete arteries. "I guess that's what you call synchronicity."

He glanced at me. "What is?"

"Salton Sea is where the CIA brought Mohammed Ben-Amini. They gave him a safe house and armed guard."

"No kidding. How'd you know that?"

"It's a long story. But I tracked him down, and I killed the bastard. Not far from Box Canyon, if memory serves."

"Son of a bitch. You hunted him down and killed him. Good man."

I nodded. "But I should have finished the job. Now Ernie is dead."

"Don't beat yourself up, mate. The job is never finished. You know that." He gave a sudden laugh. "You remember what that other Yank, Walker—Captain Walker—another crazy bastard like you. You remember what he was always saying?"

"Fearlessness is better than a faint heart for any man who would poke his nose out of doors..."

I trailed off, and he finished it. "The length of my life and the day of my death were fated long ago."

"Skirnir's Tale."

"The warrior's way, man. Ernie died doing what he was here to do, fighting the good fight. He's in Valhalla. I know that."

I studied his face as we sped through Beaumont toward Sky Valley.

"You believe that?"

"Yeah." He nodded a few times. "And so do you. I mean, I don't believe they're all in cloaks with horned helmets, quaffing beer and beating each other up, but that there is a place for warriors who fight the good fight? Yeah, I believe that." After a while, he gave me a look. "Don't fuckin' tell me you don't. Coz I know you do. It's the only way any of this bullshit makes sense!"

"Yeah?" I looked away, out at the desert. "Who says any of it makes sense?"

We came off the freeway three miles past Cactus City. Cactus City is not a city, and there are no cacti there, but I guess some bureaucrat somewhere decided it was a good name for a place in the desert.

We did a U-turn and looped under the freeway and came out onto a broad, dirt track which we followed back west and north, skirting the harsh rocky escarpments, raising huge clouds of dust on the hot air.

After maybe ten or twelve minutes of jostling and

lurching over rocks and holes, we sighted a cluster of trailers and SUVs a hundred yards off the road. As we drew closer, I spotted spotlights, microphone booms, and people milling around a clearing.

Dave pointed. "This bloody ninja is hunting me, right? He wants to kill me. So what do I do? I go into the middle of the desert, surrounded by hills, and stand listening and, get this, *feeling* the desert, waiting for him to show."

I smiled. "Feeling?"

"Yeah, like fuckin' Yoda. I told the director, Paul Grenache, we wouldn't do that. It's stupid. You know what he told me? He says, 'We're concerned with ratings, not truth.'"

"You signed up for this gig."

"Yeah, well, it was an interesting idea, right? A guy whose job is to go and kill people in really difficult situations, who has the best training there is, who's got experience of actual combat with people who actually want to kill him, right? This guy against tenth dan martial arts masters. It's a good idea." He gave a small shrug as we pulled up at the set. "I'd watch it."

We swung out of the cab, and I followed him through the milling crew toward a guy in khaki Bermudas who was gesticulating broadly and talking to a couple of guys in black T-shirts and black caps that said *CAMERA*.

He turned to Dave as we approached and smiled a smile that might have killed Cleopatra. "Dave! Nice of you to show up. Do you think maybe you can work today?" He gestured at me with both hands. "And who is this?"

It pissed me off. I said, "Why don't you ask me?"

He turned to face me. "Who are you and what are you doing on my set?"

"My name is Bauer, Harry Bauer. I was eight years in the SAS with Dave, and now I am a professional assassin. I've come to watch you get it all wrong. You have a problem with that?"

He studied my face, then Dave's, then mine again. "I guess not. Are you reliable? Do you show up on time?"

I gave a small laugh that was without humor. "All my assignments are now late. I never was. But I'm just here to watch, Mr. Grenache. I am not looking for a job."

"Shame." He put his finger on Dave's chest. "Go get ready. We have a new ninja. You upset the last one. We are shooting this bloody scene *today,* and I want a wrap!"

He walked away. I asked Dave, "Ninja?"

"Yeah. He just appears out of the sand and starts hitting me, and I'm all like, 'Whoa! What? Uh?' Bollocks. Come on. I'll show you my trailer."

FIVE

Dave was climbing in his trailer when my phone rang. It was the brigadier.

"Yeah..."

"Bradley is on his way."

"Where to? He doesn't know where we are."

"He'll call you when he arrives. He has David's address, and I've given him your cell."

"ETA?"

"This evening. He'll call you or show up. Any news?"

"No, I'm on set with Dave."

"You've spoken to him?"

"Through his hangover, yeah."

"Good. Regroup, make a plan, go on the offensive. Hunt these bastards down and kill them."

"Yes, sir."

"Keep me posted."

I told him I would, hung up, and stood watching an unintentional comedy unfold at the spot where the scene was to be shot. There was a guy dressed all in black, as a ninja. Paul Grenache, the director, was standing with him making what he probably thought were kung fu movements. The ninja was managing to look embarrassed even though he was largely invisible, and the attractive young woman standing beside him was laughing and trying to talk to Grenache. Grenache started shouting, and I heard him holler at one of the gofers to go get Dave.

I leaned my head in the door of the trailer and said, "You're on."

When he came out of the trailer, he'd changed his clothes. He had on a pair of Levis, leather lace-up boots, and a khaki military shirt. "This is the look," he said, grinning at me. Then, in what you could call a Hollywood American accent, "C'mon, boh, I'm gonna kill me some bad guys!"

I followed at a distance, observing the people milling around, trying to find someone who looked like an Afghan or an Iranian killer. The trouble is, when groups are defined by ideology, they have no special look. Ninety-nine out of a hundred jihadists might be Middle Eastern men between the ages of twelve and forty, but the one who makes a hundred might be a white, Anglo-Saxon housewife from Salt Lake City. It's not a racial thing unless there are genes for hatred and hysteria. It's a cultural, ideological thing that has been drummed into the children of Abraham for millennia: Obey, and those who do not obey, kill them.

Dave and Paul Grenache were arguing. Grenache wanted scenes that would look good on screen. Dave was arguing that when a blade kills you, you're dead before you know he's done it. While they argued, the attractive woman put her cell to her ear and walked away. She wasn't laughing anymore. She was listening carefully. I walked over to Grenache and Dave. Dave was saying, "No, sorry, mate, this is the reputation of the regiment we are talking about. If I know some geezer is out to kill me, I am not going to go out into a bloody open expanse and stand there *smelling* for him! What do you think they teach us at the—"

I put my hand on his shoulder.

"Dave?"

"What?"

"Who was the master of masters when it came to economy, speed, and brevity in combat?"

"The Duke of Wellington."

"OK, in hand-to-hand combat."

"Bruce Lee."

"And he used Tae Kwon Do for his movies, and Jeet Kune Do in combat and training. He acknowledged that Jeet Kune Do was too fast and too effective for the movies because it would all be over too fast."

I turned to Grenache. "Maybe, instead of having him standing in full view where anyone with a gun or a bow could take him out, which would be, you know, kind of stupid, you could have him using his training to move, like a mountain lion, through the undergrowth, stalking his killer. Lots of close-ups of his eyes as he watches, listens and, why not, smells the air. But the killer is a ninja, so he springs out of nowhere, and they engage in mortal combat. Plenty of Tae Kwon Do, high kicks and show, but when the time comes to finish it, you do it blade style. Swift and economical. Non telegraphing."

They both stared at me. I shrugged. "Be water, my fwend."

Grenache gestured at me with an open hand. "Listen to your friend." To me, he said, "What's your name again?"

"Harry."

"Harry makes sense. OK, we have you coming *through* the shrubs and the rocks..."

The ninja was walking away, touching his toes and doing the splits. I heard the attractive woman behind me calling Dave and Grenache. They turned, and as she arrived, she put her hand on Dave's arm.

"I am so sorry, Dave. That was the police. I don't know how close you were, but Saul, your agent, he's been found dead."

He didn't say anything. He just looked at her. I said, "What kind of dead?"

She frowned at me. "What kind of dead? The kind where you stop breathing. What kind of question is—"

"Heart attack? Road accident? Murder...?"

It was just a moment of silence, but it seemed to last a long time. Finally she said, "Murdered. Shot in the head."

"Where?"

She glanced at Paul Grenache. He gave a small nod.

"At Leo di Próvato's house. It was a big party. Everybody was there. They found Saul's body this morning in one of the bedrooms. According to the detective who spoke to me, he was sitting on a sofa, he had a box of coke and a mirror on the coffee table in front of him, and he'd been shot in the head." She turned back to Dave. "He wanted to talk to you. I told him you were with me and Paul all night and we dropped you home at four a.m. You were very drunk."

I said, "Is that true?"

"More or less. We went out for dinner. Then Dave said he wanted to go to a club."

Dave rubbed his face. "I don't remember much."

She cut in again. "Anyway, the point is we do not need this kind of publicity right now. This murder has nothing to do with Dave's background in the SAS; it is clearly related to Saul's drug habit. We distance ourselves and make a clean break."

"Who are you?"

She raised her eyebrows high on her forehead. "I might ask you the same question, pal! Except, wait, oh yeah! You're nobody, you're on my set, and you're acting like a cop. So let's start again. Who the hell are *you?*"

I sighed. "I'm Harry Bauer. I was with Dave in the Regiment. We're old friends. We look out for each other."

One of her eyebrows came down. The other arched higher. "And while you're at it, see if you can get a foot in the door in Hollywood?"

"No, thanks. Given the choice, I'd rather be boiled alive in camel piss. You said this was your set. Are you the producer?"

She hesitated a moment. "Yes, Mr. Bauer—Harry. Why are you like a cop?"

I held her eye for a long moment, thinking ahead, thinking of the variables. Then I smiled. "What's your name?"

She closed her eyes, clenched her jaw, and spoke like she was being real patient. "My name is Chelsea Granger. Now would you please tell me—"

"The Special Air Service is a regiment that is not like any other regiment, Chelsea. Aside from the very specialized training, the missions we undertake are"—I paused a moment, like I was searching for the right word—"*varied.* Some of them are military in nature, reconnaissance, sabotage, strikes, but others are closer to espionage and involve a lot of analysis and detection. So in a situation like this, training kicks in. My priority is to look out for my pal. It would be the same for him if the roles were reversed."

Her eyes were wide, and her mouth was a little slack. She said, "That is amazing. I love it." She looked at Paul Grenache. "Are you thinking what I'm thinking?"

The semi-invisible ninja spoke for the first time. He approached, shaking his head. "We have been rehearsing this scene all day, and I still haven't played it out with Dave." He pointed at Dave. "Every time we come to rehearse the scene, you're either not here, or you complain about the script, or you make some un-choreographed move. Can we just get past this scene? Can we just *do* it?"

We all stared at him. Chelsea shook her head. "Not now." She pointed at Dave. "You, Paul, and me—" She stared at me a moment. "And you. We go to the office. We talk to Sam—"

"Who's Sam?"

"Company lawyer. We prepare a statement for the cops that distances you completely from Saul's death. Then we all have lunch and we talk. We need to think in terms of a new direction."

The ninja sagged. "So do you need me *at all?*"

"Yes. Tomorrow we shoot the scene." She poked Dave on the chest. "*No more bullshit!* Let's go." To me, she said, "You follow me and Paul" like she assumed I was driving.

As we moved away, the ninja stood in front of Dave and put his hand on his chest.

"We gotta practice this fight, man. You can't keep putting me off. When are we gonna do it?"

I saw Dave's lip curl and recognized the expression. I grabbed the ninja and lifted him to one side. He wasn't real heavy.

"Go practice silent stillness, kid. We'll catch up tomorrow."

The next four hours were a waste of time carried out in various different ways. First we wasted time explaining the situation to Sam, and then we wasted time having Sam explain it back to us while I stood at his forty-eight square-foot window looking out over the spiritual desolation that is Los Angeles. Then we wasted time drafting and signing statements which Sam said he would deliver to the investigating detective.

"I loved Saul," he said at the end. "But he was a cokehead. What you gonna do? You're a cokehead, you gonna die. Cokeheads die."

I turned from the window and said, "So does everybody else."

They all stared at me. Then Sam grinned a big, loose grin and pointed at me. "He's funny. He don't talk much, but when he talks he's funny. Dry."

"Yeah, deep down funny, where it's not like funny anymore. Are we done? I have things I need to do."

They all looked at each other, raised their shoulders, and agreed they were done. Then I wasted time while Sam walked us to the elevator and everybody asked after everybody else's families.

In the elevator, Chelsea said, "Harry, I need to talk to you. Have you got half an hour?"

"No. What's it about?"

"You coming out to the set tomorrow?"

"Yes."

The elevator came to a stop, and the doors hissed open onto the parking garage. As she stepped out, she said, "It'll keep till then." Then she stopped and turned back. "Give me your number."

Two minutes later, I stood by the Jeep with Dave and watched her drive away.

He leaned against the trunk and swore softly. "She wants to give you my job."

I nodded. "I'm not surprised." I opened the doors and climbed in. He got in beside me. "You're not killing bad guys anymore, Dave. You're entertaining. You have to 'honestly expwess yourself and be water, my fwend.'"

He snorted. "You sure about that, that we're not killing bad guys anymore?"

"Nope," I said and fired up the engine. "No, I'm not."

The call came as we were headed down Santa Monica Boulevard. It was an unknown number. I pressed green and said, "Yeah."

"Montrose at Beverly Hills." Only, because he was a Kiwi, he said, "Bivirly Hills."

I smiled and took the next right. Dave chuckled. "Old Bradley." He pounded me on the shoulder with his left fist. "The Three Musketeers, mate! The Three Amigos."

I left the car outside the hotel on Hammond Street and gave the valet ten bucks and the fob. Inside we made our way through the lobby to the bar and found all six foot six of him sitting in a leather armchair, reading the LA Times and sipping a whiskey straight up. He eyed us over the edge of the paper, then dropped it on the table.

"This used to be a nice hotel. Nowadays they let any old kind of trash in."

Dave grinned. "That's how you got in, ain't it?"

The Kiwi returned the grin.

"You going to stand there giving me a pain in the neck or are you going to sit down and have a drink?"

We sat, and he told the waiter to bring a bottle of the Macallan and two more glasses. When the waiter was gone, he said, "I'm sorry about Ernie. He was a good lad."

I said, "How much did Buddy tell you?"

"The wound, the location, the scarf, and the embroidery. I don't think there's much more, is there?"

"He was looking for me there, in Pinedale. He went to see an old girlfriend of mine. She told me he said 'Del and Gabby' were looking for me. She said he told her it was my old friend Ben. But not really Ben because Ben had kicked the bucket. It was Ben's cousins, Del and Gabby."

He grunted. "Del and Gabbai, Ben-Amini's lieutenants, out for revenge. There was talk of them being in some kind of sect devoted to vengeance. Intiquaam. Anything else I need to know?"

Dave spoke up. "Yeah, my agent was shot in the head last night, at a party, while he was snorting coke."

The Kiwi frowned. "How does that tie in?"

"He was Jewish, and he was making me rich. It was set up to look like a drug-related hit. But there's no doubt in my mind, mate. He was killed because he was helping me, and he was Jewish."

"OK." He nodded. "I'll buy that." He turned to me. "You buy it?"

I nodded. "Yeah."

The waiter arrived with the whisky, poured two generous measures, and refilled the Kiwi's glass before leaving.

He took a pull, savored it, and spoke. "We don't know how many of them there are, we don't know who they are, we don't know where they are based, and we don't know what their tactics are." He paused. "We do know that they killed Ernie, we know that the manner of his execution was designed to send a message, and we know with a fair degree of certainty that they intend to take the rest of us out as punishment for the damage we inflicted on them after Al-Landy."

Dave jerked his thumb at me. "Not just that. This nutcase followed Ben-Amini to Salton Sea, where the Company had set him up in a nice house with staff and a permanent guard, and took the bastard out."

He smiled at me and arched an eyebrow. "You did that? You always were a crazy son of a bitch. Did you shove a grenade up his arse?"

He and Dave laughed. They both said, "Boomer!" and laughed some more.

I smiled, waiting for them to finish.

"We know something else. We know they are watching us and monitoring our movements. And extrapolating from that, we know they are aware that the three of us are here together. Two gets you twenty that was their intention."

The Kiwi nodded. "Agreed. So as of now we change the game. As of this moment, we are hunting them. We need intel, specifically we need to know how many of them there are, who they are, how well armed they are, and *where* they are." He nodded, as though agreeing with some inner dialogue, took a slug of Scotch, and smacked his lips. "If they deliberately brought us together, they'll regret it. No prisoners."

Dave and I nodded. "No prisoners."

The Kiwi said, "We kill them all."

SIX

WE HAD MADE A ROUGH PLAN AND WERE WORKING through the details over *fritto misto, carpaccio di manzo*, and a bottle of Barolo. Dave wasn't too happy and kept repeating that when this was all over, he still wanted his career in Hollywood. That was when my cell rang. I looked at my watch. It was just past ten p.m. I raised my eyebrows at Dave and Kiwi and answered.

"Yeah."

"Harry, this is Chelsea. Are you alone?"

"No, I'm having dinner with friends. What's the problem?"

"Can you step away from the table for ten minutes? I really need to talk to you, and I haven't got a lot of time."

I counted to ten slowly in my mind. Try it. It's a long time for the person on the other end. Then I sighed audibly and said, "OK. Will you guys excuse me a moment? I have to take this."

As I walked away from the table, I heard Dave behind

me. "He's such a wanker. Who does that? 'Will you guys excuse me? I have to take this. Bauer, Harry Bauer, shaken not stirred.'"

As I stepped out onto the sidewalk, I could hear the Kiwi laughing.

"What is it, Chelsea? If you're going to—"

"Just listen to me, will you? You can't always be right, Harry. Especially when you are basing your decision on insufficient facts."

"Wow, you sound like my mother. She used to say that every time she reached for the willow switch."

"Dave needs help."

"I know."

"Just—Harry! Just shut up for a bit. You do not need to express *every* thought that comes into your head. Just try something new and shut up and listen for a bit. OK?"

I smiled to myself, counted to seven, and said, "Can I answer?"

"One word."

"Yes."

"Good, now, Dave needs help. He's got great presence, great looks, and a great personality. The camera loves him. But he does not get that this is television. He thinks he's still in Afghanistan or Iraq and that this is real combat. Now the way you spoke to him today, what you said and how you put it across. You reached him, and he obviously respects you."

"What do you want?"

"Jesus! Buy a girl a drink! I want you to consider two things. One, be a consultant on the show for at least one season."

"A consultant..."

"It's a fancy way of saying baby-sit Dave and get him to understand what he is supposed to do on the show. We might also pick your brains about how the SAS operates and so forth. It pays well."

"OK."

This time it was Chelsea who was silent for a count of five. Then she spoke with a frown in her voice. "Really?"

"Sure. It's a great idea."

"Oh." She gave a small laugh. "Great, now here's the second part. We've discussed it, and we would love you to be a guest on the show for a couple of episodes. You and Dave, old comrades, a Yank and a Brit, fighting the forces of evil."

I sighed loudly. "Let me think about it. This is Dave's gig. I don't want him to feel like I'm muscling in."

"No, absolutely not. He's the star, the focus will always be on him."

"I'll give you an answer tomorrow."

I returned to the table and sat. I drained my wine and signaled the waiter.

"Get me an espresso and a Bushmills, straight up."

The others ordered the same, and as our plates were cleared away, I said, "She wants me as a consultant on the show."

Dave said, "Consultant..."

"Yeah, it means I baby-sit you and explain about the difference between reality and TV. See, Dave, we do want to shoot Del and Gabbai Ben-Amini and their pals, but we do *not* want to shoot Danny the Ninja."

He nodded. "Nah, you're funny. You are. Really. Dry wit. You should be on the show."

"That's what she said. Just for a couple of episodes. A Yank and a Brit united contra mundum."

"Yeah, well, we all know how that ends up, don't we?"

"Relax. I told her I'd give her an answer in the morning. Anyhow, she said you were the star. You were sexy, funny, good-looking, camera loves you."

The Kiwi was watching me closely. The waiter brought the coffee and our drinks, and as he walked away, the Kiwi spoke.

"Tell her you'll do it."

Dave sighed. "Guys, this shit will be over in a couple of weeks, and I need this show. Love you to bits, Harry, but I don't want to be looking for work as security in a club while you're gallivanting around the world replacing me on my show."

I shook my head. "Not going to happen, Dave. You're the showman. The camera loves you, not me." I turned to the Kiwi. "What are you thinking?"

"Tell her you'll do it as a two-episode special in the Wind River Mountains, Mount Freemont and Freemont Lake. You and Dave go with the crew. I'll make my own way and be waiting for you there. They'll follow us."

I nodded and grinned. "The area is notorious. People disappear up there every year, and their bodies are never found. They follow us as hunters..."

He smiled. "And they become the prey, correct. But I'm also thinking, Ernie made a point of going there. He could have called your ex, but he went there. And we're not talking about New York or LA where an Arab assassin would blend into the crowd. We're talking about Pinedale, Wyoming, population two thousand very white, Republican cowboys.

Yet this killer was unnoticed. There may be more to that than meets the eye."

I nodded. "You're right." I looked at Dave. "You OK with that?"

He narrowed his eyes at me before returning the nod. "So she said I was sexy?"

We talked some more, then the Kiwi made his way back to his hotel, and Dave and I returned to his house. There I made up a bed in a spare room, then went down to the living room and sat watching trash on the TV for four hours with the Sig in my lap.

At four a.m., Dave came down and told me, "Get some shut-eye, mate."

At seven I showered and made breakfast, and by eight we were on our way back to the set near Salton Sea.

When we arrived, the place was bustling. We parked beside Dave's trailer, and as we climbed down, I saw Chelsea approaching to meet us, and Paul, the director, hurrying behind her. He cornered Dave as he went to climb into his trailer, speaking urgently to him, "Ooooh-kaaay, now David, please, I am askin' you please, we gonna have no more games today. OK? We shoot the scene, and we gonna move on. Shoot the scene, shoot the scene, shoot the scene. Tell me!"

Dave was nodding and telling him yes. Chelsea came up to me and drew me aside toward the back of the trailer. She stood close to me and spoke quietly.

"Did you think about what I suggested?"

"Yeah, I thought about it. I'm willing to do a couple of episodes and help Dave get settled. But I am not interested in a career in Hollywood."

She smiled. "OK, that's great."

"There's one other thing."

"Tell me."

"I want to shoot those episodes in the Wind River Mountains, in Wyoming."

She frowned, and there was curiosity in her eyes, but she didn't look displeased. "Oh? Any reason?"

"Yeah, I know that area very well. The mountains are spectacular. They'd make a great setting to show off the skills and training of the SAS, which would keep Dave happy." I smiled and gave a shrug. "And it's home. I have a ranch there which I plan to open up and start breeding horses."

"In the mountains?"

"Outside Pinedale. A short drive from the Wind River Mountains and Freemont Lake. It's an ideal location for what you want to do. We've got bears, wolves, coyotes, moose, elk... You name it. People die out there every year, and their bodies are never found."

She smiled. "Sounds perfect. And you're willing to participate in the show."

I studied her face a moment and gave a small nod-shrug combination. "Sure. You might regret it. I have no skill as an actor. But I'm in for two episodes, sure."

Behind me, I heard the trailer door smack open and Dave step out saying, "Get off my back, Paul! I'll do the damned scene!"

Paul was just behind him, waving his hands in the air. "Ooooh-kaaay, I'm on *your* back. I'm the director! How can I direct if the actor ain't gonna act? I'm on your back because I askin' you—do your job! But you don't do your job. You get off *my* back and let me do mine! How's that?"

We followed them to the set. The scene had been modified to accommodate Dave's criticism that a serious Special Ops guy would not go and stand out in the open, however magnificent his profile, smelling the air for his killer. Instead he had to prowl, feline, through the desert rocks and bushes, stalking the ninja who was stalking him. There still had to be a close-up of him sniffing the air, Paul insisted, but it was just the one.

I had to smile as I watched the scene unfold. I had never expected Dave to be a good actor, but as I watched on the screen over the cameraman's shoulder, I had to admit he was good. He moved silently and with credible skill among a couple of boulders and paused. The camera closed in, and he raised his chin and sniffed the air.

"Cut!"

I glanced over at Paul. He was saying, "OK, that's a wrap! Now, Dave, I love you, come here."

I grabbed a folding director's chair and sat next to Chelsea while Paul put an arm around Dave's shoulders and another around the ninja. He was saying, "Now this is an *explosion* of action. What is the viewer gonna see? He is gonna see a close-up where you, Dave, sensin'—you *smellin'*—the killer comin' closer and closer. And *BAM!* He is on you! But we have changed that bit you don't like. Not now all the, 'Eh? What the—?' No, you are right in this. You are SAS, for Chrissakes! Right? You *explode* back—*BAM!*—and you are both lockin' in a furious, explosive fight to the death! OK?"

They both said it was OK and took up their positions. A voice cried, "*Action!*" There was a horrendous scream, and the ninja sprang onto the scene, delivering kicks and punches at a speed that surprised and impressed me.

Dave had seen enough hand-to-hand combat in actual life and death situations that his responses were real and believable, and I had to admit the fight did not look or feel choreographed. So much so that I began to wonder if they were actually going for it. But Paul shouted, "*Cut!*" and they both stopped.

Dave laughed, and so did the ninja, and they shook hands and embraced. I heard Dave say, "You're good, you son of a bitch!"

Paul was laughing as he approached. "I love it! I *love* it! Now this is the scene where the ninja is pullin' the knife, makin' several terrifying lunges and cuts, actually drawin' the blood, and then you gonna disarm him and kill him. We all clear?"

They said they were, and everyone took up their positions. Paul cried, "*Action!*" and Dave delivered two powerful hooks to the ninja's floating ribs, followed with a right hook to the jaw that sent the ninja sprawling. If the fight had been real, the ninja would have been unconscious and possibly dead, but this was Hollywood, and those blows just made him mad. In one fluid movement, he sprang to his feet and pulled a glistening tanto from his robes. Chelsea whispered to me, "*I love it!*"

The ninja slashed a big X in the air, then lunged forward. I saw his left hand go behind his back as Dave sidestepped and seized his sword arm. Then, as if from nowhere, the Ninja had a streaming scarf in his left hand. He swirled it, and it was around Dave's face. I stood. Dave clawed at the cloth, and in a microsecond, the ninja was behind him. The ninja roared. Dave made a horrible noise, and I saw the point of the tanto protrude from his chest. The ninja spun him, and now I could see the scarf, the keffiyeh, with the embroidered word *Intiquaam* impaled by the short sword.

I was already running with my P226 in my hand. My brain was struggling to make sense of what was happening. The ninja was embracing Dave, who was sagging in his arms. Then there was the grotesque, flat smack of a detonation in the air, and Dave and the ninja were torn apart in a horrible explosion of blood and gore.

I stopped dead and heard Chelsea scream behind me. The smoke and dust cleared, and there was Dave, my friend, lying twisted inhumanly, almost severed at the waist. His killer lay beside him, equally mangled.

Voices were screaming and shouting around me. The words *nine-one-one* were repeated over and over. But a voice in my head kept telling me this was not an emergency. It was already too late.

Three hours later, I sat on the step of Dave's trailer, watching the figure of the sheriff of Imperial County walk away. He had stood over me in his khaki uniform, chewing gum with his thumbs in his belt.

"I been told not to question you, Mr. Bauer."

I watched him a moment, squinting against the early sun. He seemed to be waiting for something.

"Are you waiting for an answer?"

"I don't like people getting killed on my patch, on my watch."

"You're funny that way, huh?"

"You a smartass, Mr. Bauer?"

"Are you questioning me, Sheriff?" I pointed over at the group of technicians, the director and Chelsea. "Those people will be able to give you a detailed account of what happened. If you have any doubts about your instructions, I suggest you take them up with the Pentagon."

He narrowed his eyes and spat elaborately in the dust. "You watch your step, Mr. Bauer—"

He was about to tell me what might happen if I didn't watch my step. I was getting bored, so I interrupted him.

"I think I'll watch yours instead, Sheriff. Take the right ones, and I'll introduce you to my friends in Washington. I'm pretty sure there's a lot they would like to explain to you about how law and order works in this country." I paused. His small eyes registered something like worry. I added, "Was there anything else, Sheriff?"

That was when he turned and walked away. As I watched him, I called an encrypted number. A deep New Zealand voice seasoned in tobacco and whiskey said, "Yes?"

"Dave won't be coming."

"How'd it happen?"

"The ninja."

He swore softly. "We should have seen that coming."

"Yeah. It was too obvious. They're two for two."

"You coming to the mountains?"

"Yeah. I'll let you know the details. Destroy your phone."

"Stay alive."

"You too."

I hung up and stood and made my way over to Chelsea, where she stood with the group. She turned to face me. Her eyes and nose were red from crying. She put her arms around me and held me. After a moment, I held her too and fought the lump in my throat. I had lost a lot of friends over the years, seen a lot of friends get killed in brutal ways. They tell you you get hardened to it, like growing a callus. It's a lie. Each one hurts a little more than the last. It's cumulative, and over time, it becomes intolerable.

I had once asked a Buddhist monk how to cope with that cumulative pain of loss. He had smiled and nodded, as though at a familiar question. Then he'd looked away at a small fountain that was playing nearby.

"Do you know why your friends die?" he had asked me. The question had seemed stupid at the time, and I had told him, "Yes. They die because they are killed by our enemies."

He'd shaken his head and looked me in the eye. "No, Harry. They die because they are alive. We all die in time. And we die because we are alive."

I held Chelsea and told myself Dave had died not because he had been stabbed and blown in half with a grenade, but because he was alive, and everything that is alive must eventually die. I held her tight and fought back the tears.

After a time she pulled back and looked up into my face. "Take me home."

I gave her a stupid smile that had more to do with the gaping hole in my gut than what she had asked me to do. I said, "To Wyoming?"

A small wet laugh. "Wouldn't that be nice." Then, "Where are you staying? Are you at a hotel?"

"I was staying at Dave's. I need to be there to let the guys from the consulate in. The Regiment is taking charge of his stuff. You won't want to be there."

She put her hands on my chest, then leaned her forehead on her hands.

"Take me there. Anywhere. Just get me away from here."

THEY HAD BEEN AND GONE. They had cleaned the place up, and the brigadier's men had collected Dave's stuff and taken it away. Now I stood at the French windows. They were open onto the backyard and the pool, where dusk had passed but night had not quite settled in. In the pool, the lights winked on, translucent under the turquoise ripples. There was an inflatable mattress, drifting, making a strange, dark silhouette.

But all I could see in my mind was Dave's mangled body in the dust. I searched his face, his limbs, his torn torso. They were all so familiar. I searched for him, but he wasn't there. I took a pull on my whiskey, putting that thought out of my conscious mind, and turned to look at Chelsea. She was watching me from the sofa.

I said, "I don't want you to kill the show."

She watched me for a long moment, then gave a small, wet laugh. "You don't? Well, we have a small problem, Harry." Her voice was strained, fighting back another flood of tears. "Dave is—he's not with us any longer. We have no leading man. Because—" She stopped herself, then went on, "He was unique, a one-off. He was for real, and the camera loved him."

I took a couple of steps closer and stood over her. She was looking up into my face, like she was pleading for me somehow to fix the nightmare she was living through, to make it so what had happened was no longer real. I said, "One thing they drum into us in the Regiment, until it's a part of the fabric of who we are: if you are going to survive, you have to face the facts and be ruthless."

"What are you telling me?"

"Use what happened. Use it to promote the show. This is for real. It isn't fiction. It's exactly what Dave was always demanding: Make it real. Well, this is real. Use his murder to promote the show, and use his best friend, his comrade in arms, as a stand-in to continue Dave's dream and his fight."

Her eyes were bright. "You?"

"Maybe I can't act and maybe the camera won't love me as much as it loved him, but if what we're highlighting is the reality, that won't matter so much. I'll play it straight, and Dave and his vision will be the real stars of the show."

She gave her eyes a quick wipe with the backs of her wrists. "The camera likes you just fine, Harry. Are you serious about this?"

"I'm serious. I want the show to go ahead in his name, in his honor."

"You *are* sentimental." She gave another damp little laugh. "You are one big bag of contradictions, aren't you?"

I didn't smile. "I don't know," I said. "I'm just a brute. You're the intelligent one. Why don't you tell me?"

She regarded me through narrowed eyes, wiped her tears away on her forearms again, then said, "I might have to run some tests and see just how much of a brute you are." Her breathing had quickened. She stood up, just a couple of inches away from me, and pulled off her dress.

Outside, the darkness closed in.

SEVEN

THE ARRANGEMENTS TOOK A LITTLE OVER A WEEK. It was a surreal week of meetings at the production company's offices, fifteen stories above downtown LA, with Paul and Chelsea and a team of script writers, all discussing the best way to convert Dave's murder into a ratings success.

I made it clear to them what I wanted and that the terms were not negotiable. It had to be in the Wind River Mountains in Wyoming. It had to be a small team who should be aware of the dangers and willing to face the risks—aware that Dave had been murdered. I also insisted that the martial arts experts I was to face had to be flown in later, by helicopter, when those aspects of the episodes dealing with survival in the wilderness had already been shot. I figured, privately, that would give Del and Gabbai, Mohammed Ben-Amini's nephews, time to find me and make their move. Naturally, that part of the deal was known only to the brigadier, the Kiwi, and me. I don't doubt the production company would have gone with it all the same. After all, what was a couple of lives against a massive jump in ratings? But still, we kept it private.

The truth was the whole thing nauseated me. Televising murder in a reality show to sate the lust of the lowest in human beings was not what I had signed up for, either at the Regiment or at Cobra. But what I had told Chelsea was true. It is branded into every blade's consciousness: if you are under fire and your best friend is lying next to you dead, use his body for cover. Then you kill the bastards who killed him. The last bit was my own personal addendum to the golden rule.

At our last meeting, the film crew was dispatched in a truck to establish first base at the Jackalope on Pine Street, at the exit of town, while everybody else started issuing instructions to their secretaries to book flights and hotels. I stood and grabbed my jacket and moved for the door. Chelsea intercepted me with a hand on my arm.

"I'll see you up there," I told her. "I'm going to drive up, take my time, and think things over."

There was anxiety in her eyes. Her voice was barely audible over the scraping of chairs, the shouts, and the chatter. She just said, "Come with?"

I studied her face a moment, thinking. Her cheeks flushed, and she looked away. "I'm sorry. I'm being needy."

I shook my head. "No."

Now as well as flushed cheeks, she had bright, angry eyes. "No *what?* No I can't come? That's fine!"

"No, you're not being needy. It would be nice to have you along. It's a fifteen-hour drive, if you stick to the speed limit. It'll give us time to get to know each other."

Now she looked confused but still mad. "Are you sure that's something you want to do?"

"Yeah. It's something I am sure I want to do."

"Oh." She shrugged and gave a smile you could describe as sheepish. "OK. If you're sure."

I packed a bag, locked up Dave's bungalow, and picked her up at her house. She slung three bags in the back of the Jeep, and we headed off on I-15 toward Las Vegas, Utah, and eventually Wyoming.

The drive was long and tedious, and we reached Hurricane in Utah at eight p.m. There we stopped at a motel, gassed up, and ate a pizza in the motel bedroom. Despite what we'd said, we didn't talk much, and we didn't get to know each other all that well.

We left early the next day, and by midmorning, we had come off I-80 onto Route 189 headed north through the beautiful, sagebrush wilderness of Wyoming. By lunchtime, we entered Pinedale, crossed the bridge over Pine Creek, and were soon on Pole Creek Road, climbing the dusty track toward my cabin, overlooking the great sweeping plain at the foot of Half Moon Mountain. Beyond it, the Wind River Mountains rose majestic, touched with luminous snow and dominated by Freemont Peak.

I killed the engine, and she climbed out of the car and made her way onto the deck, where she stood looking across the valley. I stood by her side, and she leaned her head on my shoulder.

"It's just—what?—seven or eight hundred miles, but it's like a different world." She pointed. "What's this flat-topped hill here?"

"That's Half Moon Mountain, and just the other side is

Half Moon Lake, and the peaks that rise beyond it are the Wind River Mountains. The big peak you can see, that looks like a saddle? That's Freemont Peak, and at the foot of that is Freemont Lake. There are lots of bodies that have gone into those mountains, and into that lake, and have never been heard from again."

"That's where we're going?"

I nodded. "I want to work out the route, but I guess we'll go via the Sacred Rim trail and then push in deeper, into the mountain above the lake."

She leaned against me and held my arm. "I'm hungry. Shall we make some lunch?"

The next few hours were spent with Chelsea on the telephone organizing the first trek into the mountains and me working out in the gym in my basement and taking a run around the ranch to get my lungs used to the mile and a half altitude. There is not a lot of oxygen at that altitude, and your body needs to make the most of what it gets.

If the previous couple of nights she had been distant and unavailable, that night she came on strong and was hard to resist. I didn't even try. Some things are like oxygen: When they are scarce, you have to make the most of what you can get. And for a few hours, I was able to pretend that what was happening meant something.

It was at four a.m., while I was lying spent but unable to sleep, staring at the starlit glow of the window, when I heard movement outside. It was not unusual for moose to come up to the house to eat the willows that grew along the banks of the stream. But moose have a particular, broken rhythm to their movements which was absent from these noises, which were not rhythmic but were purposeful.

I slipped out of bed, took the Sig from the bedside table, and moved to the window. There was no moon, but there is very little light pollution around Pinedale, and the starlight was bright. Below I could see my drive, the corner of the stables, and the willows along the river. I could not see a moose. There seemed to be no movement down there at all.

There are people who, faced with a situation like that, go back to bed. Those people tend to wind up dead. I pulled on my jeans, tucked the weapon in my waistband, and went silently downstairs.

At the bottom, I hunkered down in the shadows and listened. There was that absolute, dark silence you get in sleeping houses. But if you listened with care, there were noises behind and within the silence. A scrape, a soft crackle, a tread. Sounds no moose ever made. Sounds men make when they creep.

I moved farther into the room, keeping low by the thick wooden column that supported the roof. From that position, I had the kitchen door on my left and the plate glass French windows ahead of me. A moment longer told me the noise was coming from there. I moved closer, pressed myself against the wall beside the sliding doors, and pulled the Sig from behind my back.

There was a soft footfall on the deck outside the glass. Then the sound of a tool working at the latch. I could have shot him through the glass, but two things stopped me. I wanted him inside where I could take my shot without killing him, and also, as the thought crossed my mind, I saw the darkness of a shadow on the stairs across the room.

Then there was the whisper, *"Harry...what is it...?"*

I raised my finger to my lips, but that was as far as I got.

The latch clicked, loud in the darkness, and the door slid open three feet. A big, dark body moved in and stood motionless. It was no more than a fraction of a second, but it was all I needed. I smashed the butt of the Sig into his kidneys. He grunted and staggered forward, and I delivered a savage kick to his backside. A kick well delivered to the backside can be crippling and debilitating.

He cried out in pain, and for a second I was distracted as Chelsea raced down the stairs out of the shadows and into the kitchen. The guy was a pro, and he was tough. Because that distraction was all he needed. He lashed out a backhander with his left hand and caught me on my left ear. It grazed me but didn't hurt. He followed with a brutal right hook. I ducked, and it skimmed over my head. I closed and delivered a left and right hook of my own to his lower belly, but he was backing up, and I missed. I sprang in a fencing lunge and smacked a straight right into his chest that hurled him against the breakfast bar and sent the stools flying.

I closed in again, but this guy was made of boiled leather. A front kick caught me just above the thigh and sent me back. He came after me, and I saw the glint of steel in his right hand. The decision was instant. The time for trying to wing him and have a chat was over. You don't play games with a guy this tough in a dark house when he has a knife. He was three feet away when I pulled the trigger. The world exploded, and he stopped in his tracks. Then very softly said, "*Ya rab...*"

I backed up, holding the weapon out in front of me and snapped at Chelsea, "Put on the light!"

For a second she did nothing, then she screamed like a thing possessed, surged across the six feet separating her from the guy, and collided with him. He took one painful gasp and dropped to the floor. She backed away a couple of steps, letting out small, spasmodic screams. I spoke half to myself, asking, "What did you do?" I reached over beside the French doors and flipped the switch.

He was a big guy. He was on the floor, looking like a black heap. He was crumpled, half face down. He had black jeans, a black sweatshirt, a black balaclava over his face and head, and a large kitchen knife sticking out of his back.

I frowned at her. She was staring, rigid, at the dead lump on the floor. She kept saying, "He was—he was—" She shifted her gaze to my face. "I had to! He had a knife. He was going to kill you." Her hands went to her mouth. "What's going on, Harry? Who are these people?"

I shook my head. "You want to go back to Los Angeles?"

Her face said she was shocked. "*No! Are you kidding?* Do you know what this will do to the ratings? Are you going to call the sheriff?"

I didn't answer her, except to say, "Don't touch the body."

She backed off into the kitchen, pulling something from her back pocket while I sprinted upstairs and got my cell. As I went down, I was calling the brigadier, and I saw she was talking on the phone. I scowled at her. "Who are you talking to?"

She mouthed back at me, "*Nestor, the cameraman.* Nestor, listen, I need you here ten minutes ago, before the sheriff arrives. OK? Do it *now!*"

As she hung up, I said, "Sir, we had a visitor. I am going to have to call the sheriff. He is dead, yeah. All in black with a balaclava. He said, 'Oh, God,' in Arabic just before he died.

We haven't touched anything, but I am going to have to call the sheriff in the next couple of minutes."

His voice was crisp and alert. Like he had not been sleeping at 4 a.m. "Yes, good. One less. Call the sheriff, I'll take care of everything. If he gives you trouble, have him call me."

I said I would and called the sheriff's office. I spoke to a deputy .

"Good morning. I have a home invasion. I shot the guy, and he is dead. I think you'd better alert Sheriff Levi. He will want to know about this, and I need to talk to him."

He asked me for my name and address and said a couple of cars and the sheriff were on their way.

An hour later, Seth sat out on the decking with us as the early light filtered over the Winds in the east. He had an untouched mug of coffee on a log by his side. Chelsea was sitting in a rocking chair with a blanket around her shoulders nursing a mug of her own. Seth was shaking his head and narrowing his eyes at me.

"Harry, I thought you weren't coming back. You told Doc Erickson you weren't coming back. I'm going to be straight with you, Harry. Whatever friendship we may have takes second place. I don't want you bringing this shit into my town."

Chelsea glanced at me. "Who's Doc Erickson?"

I ignored her and nodded quietly for a moment. "Everything takes second place for somebody, right, Seth? Have they been in touch with you from DC yet?"

"Yeah." He sighed and looked out at the dawn. "Yeah, they called me from DC. They told me somebody would be coming for the body and to hand it over to them. They told me to stay out of your way but help if you needed it." He shook his head. "I can't believe, after everything that happened with you and Claire, that you are bringing this shit into our town."

"I'm not."

Chelsea said, "Who's Claire?"

"Nobody."

Seth said, "Excuse me?"

"I am not bringing this into your town, Seth. I am taking it out to the Winds. And with a bit of luck, you will never see me"—I jerked my head at the ambulance where the body had been taken on a gurney—"or them again."

Seth pointed at Chelsea. "What about this young lady? Will we ever see her again, or are you going to leave her stacked with all the other bodies to be eaten by the coyotes and the bears?"

"She doesn't care, Seth. She works in television. All she cares about is her ratings."

He let out a deep, unhappy sigh and went to stand. "Is there anything you want from me?"

I shook my head. "No. Just stay away, don't get hurt, and look after whoever you have to look after." I locked my eyes on his. "You stay safe."

He nodded. He stood and took a step off the deck toward his RAM. There he stopped and turned, frowning at us both.

"You stabbed him and shot him, both at the same time?"

I didn't answer, but Chelsea said, 'I thought he was going to kill Harry. He had a knife. I just acted without thinking."

"So you stabbed him."

"And at that same moment Harry fired his gun. It was all so quick…"

I said, "Seth…"

He sighed. "Yeah, OK. I hope you grow out of this some day, Harry."

"Me too."

He climbed in his truck, and I watched the taillights follow their unsteady path down the driveway, toward the road. The ME followed, and the deputies went after him, and pretty soon, we were alone.

That was when she turned and looked inside and said, "Did you get all of that?"

Then the voice from the shadows, "*Oh-my-God!* Did I? Did I get it? Chelsea, darling, this changes *everything! Everything!*"

Nestor came out onto the decking holding his micro camera. Chelsea jumped up to look over his shoulder. I stood and walked away. I felt suddenly nauseous. I had to wonder sometimes how much difference there was between the people I had hunted and killed for Cobra and the people we were supposed to be protecting. They all seemed at times to be driven by a fundamental lack of humanity.

I came around the house and stopped to look across the sweep of the plain. The glow of the sun was rising behind the Wind River Mountains. Against the glow, they soared, setting their snowy peaks high in the sky, so that they seemed to be not of this Earth. As though they were a gateway to another place—to that other place.

Death was up there, waiting. Waiting for me.

EIGHT

WE SET OUT LATE, SKIRTING THE TOWN PAST THE museum of the Mountain Man and the Pinedale Clinic where, in another life, it seemed, in another world, once-upon-a-time, I had met Doc Erickson, and she had given a damn. We climbed past the cemetery where desultory stars and stripes mourned the passing of men and women who had given their lives for their country: for America, for an ideal they believed in, for a dream.

"Cynics," I said, half to myself. "They believe fighting for dreams is a stupidity. That dreams are not worth fighting for."

She turned to look at me like I had just charged her from left field. In the back, in the shadows, I could feel Nestor filming. I fought the impulse to rip the camera from his hands and shove it where he'd need a flash to get a picture of his breakfast.

Chelsea said, "I had you down as a cynic. You're telling me you think dreams are worth fighting for?"

"They're the only thing worth fighting for," I half-snarled. "What?" I gestured out of the window in disgust. "This reality is worth a fight? Democracy? An ever more subjugated, obedient hive? Freedom? A set of ever more limited, qualified rights granted by an ever more despotic set of elitist minorities! The pursuit of happiness? The happiness an algorithm assigns you based on its analysis of your use of the Internet. Shall I go on? Is this dystopian reality worth a fight?" I shook my head. "No. Only dreams are worth fighting for. Especially the dream that one day human beings might actually be smart enough to wake up and realize that democracy is making your own damn choices, that freedom is making your own damn choices, and you pursue happiness by making your own damn choices."

An uncomfortable silence permeated the cab as we crested the hill and moved along the east side of Freemont Lake.

After a couple of minutes, Chelsea glanced over her shoulder. She was asking if he had filmed it, and I heard him whisper he had. A brief but profound depression gripped me for a few moments. This, these two people riding with me in the Jeep, they represented my North Star. Had this really been was what I was defending when Ernie and Dave and the Kiwi and I had gone after Ben-Amini and his cousins and slaughtered them in their dozens?

"Is this it?" I asked, and regretted it as I spoke but could not stop. "Is this it? Is this the big battle? Is this what we are fighting for? The right to take real, three-dimensional, visceral human pain, squash it into two dimensions, and feed it to hundreds of millions of people—maybe billions of people, as the closest they are ever going to get to actual reality? All the rush with none of the pain. And somebody the camera likes to take the role of you."

I looked at Chelsea. She was watching me like she was watching a movie. I saw her eyes flick at Nestor in the back seat and felt for a moment like I was trapped like a rat in a maze.

Or a hive.

"This is what it boils down to? This is what these guys gave their lives to protect and defend? Our right to take the third dimension out of reality and stream it under the pretense that this is the closest they, they Great Gray Mass, can ever get to true reality. That's our big dream, what we live and die for. It's Vegas and Tinsel Town on fucking steroids."

"I thought you wanted to do this." It was Chelsea.

"You did?"

"You said you wanted to do it."

I grunted. "Yeah. I said I wanted to do it. I want to do it."

"So what are you griping about? Where's all this suddenly coming from?"

"I want to do it," I said. "I'm just not sure why anymore."

We drove on in silence, with the lake, vast and dark, on our left. Nestor's cell rang once, and he talked for a while on the phone in Spanish.

"They settin' out late, like us," he said after a while. "They said we godda wait for them at the trailhead, and they gonna find us and join us."

Nobody answered him. Soon we began to climb toward the White Pine Resort, and Chelsea said suddenly, "I think it's because you don't want your friends' deaths to be in vain, and I think that at heart, even if you hate what has happened to our Western society, however awful it might seem at times, it's better than the alternative, which would be forced on us if people like you were not protecting us."

I didn't answer right away because the answer I had on my lips was too ugly to speak, but as we passed the turn-off for the White Pine Resort and began to climb toward the trailhead, the words fell from my mouth, and I let them lie there, and the devil take the hindmost straggler to the dust.

"Every good man's death is in vain because it serves no purpose. I would like my friends' lives not to have been in vain. But if I am here, it is not to celebrate their lives or commemorate their deaths, it's to avenge them and exact a quart of blood for every ounce they gave.

"And as to the value of this world I fought to protect, which you think is a better alternative than Sharia Law, don't be so sure. Don't be so sure. There they beat you and torture you to bring you into submission, and sometimes the strong fight back. But in this dystopian madness you are helping to create, they just suck your soul and your will out digitally by wi-fi and leave an appropriately hive-adjusted drone where a troublesome human being used to be." I shook my head. "I am not sure which of those two alternatives is actually the most dangerous."

"Boy! You are in a real state today, huh, Harry?"

"Yeah," I told her. "I'm in a real state today."

Not long after, we pulled into the Sacred Rim trailhead and parked the Jeep. There were not many cars there. It wasn't so much that it was early in the season, as this year the winter had hung on into late May with sub-freezing temperatures and snowstorms, and even now, here and there, drifts of snow were banked up against the restrooms and tool sheds, the sides of the roads and the denser clumps of pines and undergrowth that fringed the forest.

Normally by this time of year, the bears would have retreated higher into the mountains, where it was cooler. But in years like this one, where the cold and the snow had lingered, you'd be more likely to find them at lower altitudes, sleepy, hungry, and bad-tempered. A sleepy, hungry, bad-tempered bear is not something you want to meet in a forest, or anywhere else for that matter, so the trekkers were still few this year, and those there were were mainly locals who knew the score.

I swung out of the cab and went to the back. There I buckled on my Sig and strapped my Fairbairn-Sykes to my calf inside my boot and a large bowie to my waistband behind my back. Chelsea climbed out and approached as I was clipping a pepper spray to my belt. It always struck me as ironic that out here the pepper spray was for the bears, and the semi-automatics were for hostile humans you might meet.

"What are you doing?"

I pulled over my rucksack and double-checked the supplies I had in there: night vision goggles, ammo for the Sig, extra thermal clothing for the nights, high protein bars, a spare P226, a suppressor, and four clips of six twenty-inch hunting arrows for a horn and orange Osage laminated Mongol-style bow that at a mere thirty-six inches in length had a sixty-pound draw weight and could punch a hole right through the densest skull.

"I'm going up the trail."

"We have to wait for the crew."

"You have to wait for the crew. I don't. By the time they've arrived, checked their equipment, organized themselves, and had a piss, it will be lunchtime. They're not going to be moving out till two o'clock at the soonest. I'll be back by then."

"Where are you going, Harry?"

"Why?" I pulled the rucksack on my back. "I'll see you before two."

I crossed the parking lot and started along the track east and a little north, like I was headed for the Sacred Rim, but what I was more interested in was exploring north, where the ground leveled off and then dropped steeply toward Freemont Creek Canyon, with Long Lake and Upper Long Lake on the right, to the north and east, and Lake Freemont on the left and to the south.

I had walked no more than a hundred yards or so, picking my way through the dappled foliage, over fallen trees and branches, when I heard the shout from behind me. I stopped and turned, with my right hand moving instinctively to the release catch on my holster. But it was Chelsea, running through the tall grass and the sparse saplings at the fringe of the woods with her small rucksack bouncing and all the natural grace and style of a four-hour-old colt.

"*Wait up!*"

She slowed to a slight stagger and stood bent double with her hands on her knees, breathing deeply.

"We're at well over one and a half miles in altitude," I told her. "Altitude sickness happens here. It has nothing to do with how fit you are. Running is not smart."

"No shit," she said and stood upright, breathing

through her mouth. I waited a moment, then asked, "What do you want?" She frowned. I jerked my chin back where she'd come from. "You came after me. You were running. What do you want?"

She continued to frown at me. "You know what? I came after you because I wanted to come along with you. But there is another reason too. I want to know why you are being such an asshole!"

I sighed, turned, and started walking again. She followed, trying to keep up and catch her breath.

"Are you going to answer me, or are you just going to walk in silence?"

I covered another fifty yards, stopped, and scanned the area, looking and listening. We were alone. I turned, grabbed a fistful of her collar, and dragged her in close to me. Her eyes went wide, and her cheeks flushed, but she was too breathless to cry out.

"Barely six hours ago you stabbed a man in the back and killed him. I do that for a living, and sometimes I find it hard to deal with." I looked her over from head to foot and back again. "But look at you. All you can damn well think about is ratings and catching the scene for your filthy reality TV."

I let go her collar and gave her a small shove as I did it.

"Dave was more than a brother to me. What he and I went through together—there are no words to describe that. And you—" I gestured at her. "You want to turn his death into entertainment. You kill a man, and hey! That's entertainment too." I took a step toward her. She tried to pull back and almost lost her footing on a fallen branch. I pointed savagely back toward Pinedale.

"That son of a bitch you stabbed—"

"You shot him."

"Shut up! That man had a mother, maybe he had a family, he had a history, and as much as he was a son of a bitch who deserved to die, he was also a living, breathing, suffering human being! And when you kill a human being, the normal, healthy reaction is to have some kind of emotional response! Like feel conflicted, nauseous, depressed! Not ask your cameraman if he caught it, for Christ's sake!" I stared at her a while, and she looked down at her feet, like she was five and I was her dad and I was mad. I shook my head. "Do you feel *nothing* about the fact that you killed a man this morning?"

She gave her shoulders a small twitch and raised her eyes to meet mine.

"He was going to kill you."

"I'm not—" I sighed and ran my fingers through my hair. "Chelsea, I am not asking you to justify killing him. I was about to kill him myself. He had it coming. No question." I gestured at her, shaking my head. "But you should be traumatized by what you did, and you're not. You don't care. All you care about is your damned ratings."

"And you. Maybe you didn't notice, but I killed him to save you. And I am trying rather hard to be with you, in spite of the fact that you are acting like a complete asshole."

I stared at her. After a minute, she looked away.

"Of course I feel something about what I did this morning." She was quiet for a bit. The breeze sighed and moved the branches above us. "I keep reliving what happened. He was huge. This huge shadow in the darkness. And he was moving at you, so fast. And all I could think was that he was going to kill you. Then I saw the glint in his hand, and I didn't think. I just acted. Next thing..."

She trailed off, then shook her head. "I guess I've behaved like a type-cast, stereotypic Hollywood jackass, ratings, ratings, ratings, like nothing else in the world matters. But the truth is, all I've been doing, Harry, is hiding the horror I am living through inside, and all the while, I am terrified you are just going to turn around and walk away. Or get killed. Please..." Her face crumpled, and I watched in horror as she started to cry, gave her arms a little flap, and said, "Please don't be mean to me."

And then she took a couple of stumbling steps toward me and wrapped her arms around my waist.

"Please don't leave me alone to face this." She sobbed into my chest, and I felt my shirt turn wet. "Don't leave me alone to face this..."

I rolled my eyes, gave her a few pats, and said, "Come on, let's go scout out the land. You'll feel better if we walk a bit."

In my mind, I called silently on Ernie and Dave, in an odd echo to what Chelsea had been saying to me just moments before. "You sons of bitches have left me to face this alone...!"

She wiped her eyes and then her nose on her sleeve, apologized, and we set off along the almost invisible track into the wilderness.

NINE

WE WALKED FOR AN HOUR, MOSTLY IN SILENCE, though she made enough noise with broken twigs, branches, heavy gasping for air, and pleas to stop and breathe to have alerted an entire army to our presence. But hard as I listened, and hard as I scanned the shadows and the undergrowth, I didn't detect anyone following us.

Eventually we came to an outcrop of rocks backed by pines and black cottonwood trees that overlooked the steep descent toward Freemont Creek. There I selected a spot where we were protected on three sides and had a good view of anyone climbing the hill toward us.

We dumped our sacks, and I handed her my canteen. She took a pull and sat on a rock in the shelter of the outcrop. She closed her eyes to the sun for a moment, then said, "It was my dad."

"What was?"

I sat next to her and took the canteen from her hand.

"He told me when I was six years old, 'Chelsea, if you

want to survive in this world, you have to be ruthless.'" She opened her eyes and raised a finger. "But if you want to succeed in this world, ruthlessness is not enough. If you want to succeed you have to be a ruthless predator."

I took a swig and screwed the cap back on. "You believe that?"

"No. I know it's wrong." She shook her head a few times. "Compassion, kindness, giving a damn, they are not feelings that occur in nature. Not the way we feel them. These are human constructs that we have created so that we can survive socially. So if you want to survive, and succeed, then you need to be social, you need to be kind and have compassion. That is how humans survive." She looked across at me. "Right?"

I didn't say anything. It didn't matter because she had started talking again.

"I mean, you might think, 'In a survival situation I'd rather be with your dad than with you. Compassion and empathy ain't gonna get you very far in a life-or-death situation.' Wrong! You're with my dad in a life-or-death situation, and chances are he'll kill you and eat you. But compassion and kindness will keep the both of you alive, giving each other warmth and support and cooperation." She paused a moment. "You know that."

"I do?"

"Sure, SAS, patrols of four who will not let each other down. You know that those three guys are what stands between you and death. You know each other, you understand each other, you care about each other. Am I wrong?"

"No."

"Right. My dad was an asshole. He made me kill my pet

bunny and my puppy when I was six years old, to teach me ruthlessness. My mom and I cried for a week."

"I'm sorry."

"You know?" She turned and studied me for a moment, then looked out across the valley again. "You know, when we die, we don't go to hell. We are already there. The trick of the game, the key, is to learn how to get out. I mean—" She gave a bitter laugh and tried to disguise it as something else. "I mean, what kind of god, right? What kind of god gives a six-year-old girl a father who makes her kill her pet bunny, and her puppy, just so she can learn to be ruthless? What kind of god makes a world like that?" She stared at me for a long while, and I stared back. Finally she said, "Do you know, Harry?"

I shook my head. "No, I don't know. But the whole world isn't like that."

"Yeah, I know. Hell has levels, from well beyond what any human can endure without passing out or dying, all the way to the tedium of purgatory. Each unique individual human with his own unique version of hell." She tapped her finger lightly on my knee. "And each one of us learns to hide the pain in our own unique way."

I didn't know how to answer her. After a moment, she tilted her head on one side.

"Do you let people see your hell, Harry? Or do you hide it behind your own Hollywood show? The wiseass tough guy feels no pain." She gave a sudden, startling laugh. "You blow a guy's brains out—*bang!*" She made the gesture, using her fingers as a gun. "*Bang!* Then you poke a cigarette in your mouth, lean in to the flame of a match, and pour yourself a shot of whiskey. All in a day's work."

We sat looking at each other in silence. She went on. "But nobody ever gets to see your version of hell. Because the only way you can get through, the only way you can take the next step, is by convincing everybody around you, and with a bit of luck yourself too, that you have no feelings. That inside, your heart is made of stone—life and death, pleasure and pain, it's all the same to you."

"You talk too much."

I reached for my rucksack, about to stand up. Her voice stopped me.

"But it was different this time. Something about it was different this time." I turned to look at her. "You've lost friends before. You've lost people you cared about. But this time was different."

"You done?"

"You got really mad at me. You practically accused me of being an inhuman monster. Dave's death touched you so deep that for a moment there you couldn't hide your..." She paused, staring up at the translucent green of the cotton-wood leaves. She raised her shoulders an eighth of an inch and shifted her gaze back to me. "...vulnerability?"

"You made your point, Chelsea. Stop while you're ahead."

"Is that where I am, Harry, ahead?"

I stood. "Come on, let's get back to the trucks. We have a long hike this afternoon."

She sat and watched me pull on my rucksack. When I was done, she said, "You judged me harshly. I only wanted you to see that what I do to cope with my pain is not so different than what you do."

"I got it. We have to go."

We walked back in silence. She stayed close behind me on the narrow path. I kept my attention focused on the dense undergrowth on either side of us, listening for any sound that broke the patterns. The breeze had its pattern of rustles and sighs and creaks, the birds had their patterns of flurries, swoops, flappings, and flutters. Everything in the wilderness has its pattern of sounds except the stalking predator. He creates a silence within those patterns, and he moves through that silence, closing on his prey. So if he treads on a twig, snaps a branch, upsets a rock, or scares a bird, he will break the pattern of sounds and alert an observant listener that something is moving in the silence.

But nothing broke the patterns, and we arrived back at the parking lot without incident. The truck was there beside my Jeep. The back was open, and Nestor and Paul Grenache, the director, were there with Geoff, the sound technician, and a guy I'd been introduced to as Dyno, who was all hair and tattoos.

Beside the truck was a restored VW camper which must have been at least sixty-five years old. It had been painted in the style of the Summer of Love, with a big Ban the Bomb symbol on each side and then psychedelic images of yellow submarines, golden apples, black nudes with more Afro hair than you'd think possible on one head, and much more besides.

As we approached, I saw that the kids who came with the van were hanging with Nestor and the technicians. They didn't exactly fit the part. They were too healthy, too alert, and too un-cool. If you mentioned Ginsberg to any of these kids, they'd probably ask you if he was one of Leah Remini's Scientology pals before she broke up with

Jennifer Lopez. I raised my voice above their chatter and laughter.

"We move out in one hour. Get your gear ready, and if you want to eat, eat now. Next food stop will be at six p.m."

Their chatter and laughter died down. Dyno was standing in the back of his van leaning on the side with his tattoos crossed over his chest.

"You givin' orders now, Harry?"

I stopped in my tracks and looked at him with dead eyes.

"Is that a conversation you want to have?"

He turned to Paul. Paul shook his head.

"All right, Harry, we'll be ready." Then, to the world at large, "OK, guys! Fifteen minutes for lunch and let's get cracking!"

I had a glance at the kids from the camper. They were hard to tell apart. There were three of them, and they looked like they hadn't eaten for a few weeks, but they didn't mind. They all had pale blue Levis torn at the knees, and they all had T-shirts that seemed to defy the laws of physics because though they were extremely small, still they were very loose and baggy around the biceps.

The closest one, who had a key outlined in his pocket, had thick black hair that seemed to have dropped onto his head from a height. When he parted it with his fingers to see, his eyes were blue, and he had a permanent nasal grin on his face, like, wasn't life like *funny?* Like, *all the time?*

His pal, if that's what he was, was different from the guy with the key only in that what had fallen on his head seemed to be a raccoon, and some tattoo artist had managed to find enough room on his upper arm to tattoo a skinny girl with lots of hair and a katana.

The third one appeared to be a girl, though it was hard to tell for sure. Her hair was longer and covered most of her face. She had a ring in her nose, and her hips were wider. You couldn't define any of them as masculine or feminine. It was a whole different thing they had going on.

I spoke to the guy with the key in his pocket. "You headed for Sacred Rim?"

He nodded. "Uh-huh. Is it like sacred?"

The girl said, "For like Native Americans?"

I shook my head. "No. It's not like sacred, it is sacred; and not for like Native Americans. It is sacred to Native American Indians."

Their mouths hung open in almost identical wet, pink grins. He said, "Man that's so cool." She added an inflected nuance by observing, "*Really* cool."

I gave a single nod. "The weather can change really fast up here, and this year the summer is late. You guys want to see the rim, you need to get going while the weather holds."

The kid with the dead raccoon on his head spoke for the first time.

"You like a ranger or something?"

"Yeah, I'm like a ranger, or something."

"You makin' a movie? Dyno said you was like makin' a movie or somethin'."

I looked up at Dyno. He was stuffing a burger in his mouth, caught my eye, and shrugged.

I searched the three young faces for a small spark of thought or near-wakefulness. They all looked back, waiting.

"You guys need to go. Where we are going, you can't go. There are bears, hungry and bad-tempered that can tear your limbs off and kill you in seconds. And there are sudden blizzards as evening sets in that can kill a person in less than an hour. So your best bet is to go up the trail to the rim. You guys have a good afternoon."

"Can we, like, hang out with you guys?"

"No."

Raccoon said, "I'd be like so cool, man, to see an actual *movie*..."

"No."

Chelsea appeared from the Jeep eating a sandwich and grinning. "Come on, Harry. Don't be such a grinch! You guys never saw a movie being shot?" They made affirmative noises. "This isn't exactly a movie. It's more like a reality show."

"Chelsea!"

She looked at me. "What?"

I fixed her with my eye. "We cannot have spectators on this episode. That is fine."

She scowled. "OK! Chill, will you! I'm just chatting with the guys. Go get something to eat. You're like Mother Goose, for cryin' out loud!"

I went and got some food, double and triple-checked my rucksack, and went and sat on a fallen tree, looking up into the forest. I could hear Chelsea and the crew talking and laughing with the kids. It had that dull, damp echo you get in forests, resonant yet muted. I listened for other sounds, searched for movement. Right then, in that moment, I was the prey—the bait. As soon as I felt the line tug, as soon as I knew they had bitten, I would become the predator. Until then, I had to watch and wait, and listen.

Half an hour later, the crew were kitted out and fed, and I led the way into the deep green light of the forest. We had advanced north a ways and then turned west and started the descent toward Freemont Creek when a noise behind me caught my attention. I stopped and turned. Chelsea was immediately behind me. She stared into my face and said, "What?"

Over her shoulder, I could see Paul, the director, talking animatedly with Nestor. Trailing behind him were Dyno and Geoff, the sound technician. My heart sank at the sight. We were sitting ducks, and I prayed to whatever god deals with this shit that the Kiwi had his eye on us.

But what really gave my stomach a twist was the three kids trailing us. I scowled at Chelsea and pointed at them. "What are they doing?"

She shrugged. "They said they wanted to come and watch us shoot the episode."

"Are you out of your mind? Did you not see what happened to Dave? Do you not understand what is happening here?"

"For Christ's sake, Harry! It's a *reality* show! You take what comes along and you ingrate—"

I pushed past her and made my way back toward the kids. I passed Paul and Nestor and Dyno and Geoff. They glanced at me as I went by, and after a moment I heard Chelsea's voice and scattered laughter.

The kids saw me approach and slowed to a halt. I pointed at the guy with the keys in his pocket.

"What's your name?"

"Kai."

I frowned. "Kai?"

"It's Navajo. It means Willow."

"You're Navajo?"

"No."

I gave up and turned to the kid with the raccoon on his head.

"What's your name?"

"September." He gave a small shrug. "I was born in September."

I turned to the girl. "I guess it's too much to ask that you're called Jane."

She frowned like I was crazy. "Who's called Jane these days? My name's Allivya?"

She made it sound like a question. Like she wasn't sure I understood she was called Allivya. I gave a single nod.

"OK, Kai, September, and Allivya, you guys need to turn around and go away, as far from here as you possibly can. You understand me? You need to go."

It was Kai who answered. "We want to watch you making your movie."

I stepped up close to him. He looked up into my face. There was an obstinacy there. I spoke in something between a snarl and a whisper.

"If you stay, you will all three die. Leave. Now."

TEN

WE COVERED JUST THREE MILES, BUT WE HAD NO path to follow, and we were moving down an increasingly steep gradient. In addition, we were weaving in our tracks, seeking places where Paul and Nestor could get good footage of the environment to show just how remote and isolated it was. A couple of times they had me stand against the wild backdrop and look menacing, and once Paul had me hunker down with the hunting knife in my hand and say, "You kill a man out here, and his body is never found."

When I was done, he grinned at me.

"That's good. Most guys, we'd have to do multiple takes because they'd laugh at a line like that, you know, trying to sound serious. You was perfect first time, man."

He looked up at Chelsea, nodding. She was nodding back.

I stood. "It's not a funny line, Paul. It's true."

By the time we reached first camp, on the north shore of Lake Freemont, where Pine Creek empties into the lake, the sun was slipping behind the Freemont Ridge to the south and west, and the air coming off the lake was cold.

We pitched our tents. There were four of them. Geoff and Dyno shared one, Nestor shared another with Paul, and Chelsea and I shared a tent. The fourth was a storeroom for the equipment.

By then it was too late to hunt or fish, so Geoff and Dyno set about making a fire and preparing a meal from the supplies we had brought with us. They looked like they knew what they were doing, so I left them to it, though I had to admit the smell from the flames and the crackling wood was a damned sight better than the smell coming out of the pot.

By nine o'clock, we had all gathered around the fire. The sun was gone, and the chill coming off the water was enough that we had brought our blankets and wrapped ourselves in them within the flickering circle of warmth. I had also hung the night vision goggles around my neck, under my blanket.

Dyno, who had assumed the role of cook for that night at least, ladled out a kind of thick stew containing canned beef stew, canned meatballs, small chunks of salami, and canned potatoes. It should have been disgusting, but after an exhausting day of walking in the mountains at that altitude, it tasted delicious. We ate in silence until all you could hear was the spoons scraping the remains from each bowl.

Paul laughed suddenly. It was startlingly loud in the wilderness.

"That was good! Huh? Was that good?"

Dyno chuckled. "Secret ingredient to any meal, makes it gourmet quality and never fails—hunger!"

Everybody laughed. Nestor lay back with his head on his

rucksack. "Man, has anybody looked up at these stars? When was the last time any of us saw stars like these?" He lifted his head and looked across at me. "OK, not you, Harry. I know you see stars like this pretty often. But the rest of us...*man!*"

We all looked up. There was no moon. So the sky, instead of the translucent turquoise you get sometimes with a bright moon, was almost black, and the stars—billions of them—seemed to be smeared across the dome of the sky like shaved ice, peppered with microscopic diamonds, twinkling blue, red, and gold. It was Dyno who spoke.

"You often see skies like this, Harry? In Iraq and Afghanistan?"

"Sure. I also come out here to hunt sometimes. I might spend three or four days..." I trailed off and pointed up at the mountains behind us. "Up there, the air is even thinner and cleaner. The stars you see up there are not like anything you've ever seen anywhere else."

"How long were you in Special Forces?"

I studied his face. Everyone had gone quiet, watching me. He was obviously asking the questions everybody else wanted the answers to. Far off, an owl cried out.

"Eight years."

The fire crackled. A constellation of sparks rose suddenly on the hot air and trailed down toward the water. Dyno tossed a twig into the flames. "I've seen the night sky in Iraq and Afghanistan. I wasn't Special Forces. Nothin' like that. I was just a grunt who could fix things. But I have some questions. I think we all have. That OK?"

"I guess that depends on the questions."

Nestor had pulled himself back into a sitting position, with his elbows hugging his knees.

"They gave us the option, after Dave was killed. We can pull out, or we can accept danger money, because it was a high risk job. Of course, they gonna incorporate that into the spin for the show, but we know it's real because we seen, all of us here, we seen what happened to Dave. So we accepted, for the money, and because by now we are committed, right? But still, we got questions."

I smiled at him to take the edge off. "You going to ask me the questions or just tell me you got them?"

Dyno said, "What happened to Dave?" He sighed and raised both hands. "I was there. I saw what happened to him. What I'm asking, what I think we would all like to know, is *what happened?* How could a thing like that... Who did that to him?"

I looked down at the dust, seeing Dave's severed body lying in the dirt, away in California.

"How many questions is that?"

"Just one, Harry. And you know what I am asking. We are all here, in the mountains where you wanted to bring us. We have a right to know."

I nodded and gave a small laugh through my nose.

"I'll answer your question as best I can. But before that, let me tell you all something for free. Rights are something politicians made up so people would stop thinking about their liberties. A right is something your government allows you to do or have. Without them, you ain't shit. Liberties are things you can do, unless the government tries to stop you. So have you got a right to know what happened to Dave?" I shook my head. "No, that's not written anywhere. But I'll tell you what I can."

I could feel the warmth of the flames on my skin. They

were all watching me closely. My words had resonated with them, but they hadn't liked them much. I took a deep breath and felt myself drawn back through the years to another place, another fire under the desert stars.

"Dave and I, and a couple of other guys, we formed a kind of vigilante group in Afghanistan. We got sick of watching families get massacred for playing music at a wedding. We got tired of watching villages of men, old guys, women and children, raped, tortured, and massacred for watching TV. We watched one too many of these acts of barbaric evil, and we went on the offensive. We went out and we tried to avenge the thousand and one victims."

I paused, watching the shadows waver behind the gathered circle.

"It was too late for the dead. It is always too late for the dead. But the next time some son of a bitch went to rape a child, he might pause and remember what happened to his friends last week, and think twice."

Dyno asked, "Was this in Afghanistan?"

"Yeah. By the time I left, we had wiped out almost an entire clan, run by a guy called Mohammed Ben-Amini. There was just him, his two nephews, Del and Gabbai, and a handful of men, out of maybe five hundred men. I found Ben-Amini, and I killed him with my own hands. But we never got to Del and Gabbai. And they have come after us seeking vengeance."

"Holy *shit!*" It was Geoff, speaking for the first time. He stared at Chelsea with wide, angry eyes. "Did you know about this?"

She drew breath, but I cut across her. "Nobody knew about this except me and Dave."

Geoff raised his voice. "Let her answer for herself!"

I spoke very quietly. "Why don't you make me, Geoff?" I held his eye while it dawned on him how stupid he had been. When he swallowed, I said, "When you made the decision to come, you knew as much as the producers and the management team. If anybody has used you, it has been me. There is a team hunting me right now. They are out there"—I jerked my chin out at the darkness—"and I have used you and your company to draw them out here, into my territory. Here I will hunt them, and I will kill them, and nobody will ever find their bodies.

"Tomorrow you can either stay, if you think you can make something of it, or you can leave. I will be going out there." I pointed up into the mountains. "I will disappear, and you won't be able to film what I do. But I will draw the danger away from you."

"Oh, thanks a lot! That's real big of you. Having drawn us into a death trap surrounded by crazy jihadists, he courageously leads the killers away! I mean, couldn't you have just come on your *own?* Wasn't that an option also?"

"No, Geoff, or I would have done it. There was no way to guarantee they would know where I was going, or that they would follow, unless I made a big show of it. This was the obvious way. You all saw what happened to Dave, you all knew the risk." I gave a small laugh and shook my head. "What are you saying, that getting blown in half by jihadists is somehow worse than getting blown in half by a jealous husband or a jilted lover? The risk hasn't grown any greater because now you know they are jihadists, Geoff. You chose to take the risk and get paid for it."

He muttered an obscenity under his breath, but before I

could answer, a scream ripped through the darkness. Dyno blurted, "*What the—*"

Geoff and Nestor scrambled to their feet, turning to stare out into the blackness. Paul did a weird crab-dance across the circle, whimpering, "*Chelsea? Chelsea?*"

I shouted, "*Get down! Stay put! Form a ring!*" To Dyno, I snarled, "You know what to do. *Do it!*"

Then I sprinted out of the circle of light. I could hear Chelsea's voice ringing out behind me, "*Harry!*" but I was already gone on silent feet, hunkered down with the night vision goggles turning the world into a stygian blackness inhabited by dancing green demons. I kept low, partly to avoid making a silhouette, partly to cast any oncoming figures against the horizon.

The scream tore out again, directly ahead of me. Now it was accompanied by the crashing and stumbling of a heavy body moving through undergrowth and falling on loose rocks. Now I could see the flickering green of a warm body moving fast through the blackness of the trees and the bushes.

Another scream. I had no doubt now that it was female. I moved, crouching, on rapid, silent feet to intercept it.

She burst out of the trees like a green fire-demon, screaming, "*Help me! Oh Christ! Help me! Please help me!*"

I stood, reached out, clapped my hand over her mouth, hugged her tight, and took her to the ground. She whimpered and thrashed until I snarled in her ear, "*Shut up!*"

She froze.

I whispered, "*I told you not to follow us. Remember? I'm the miserable asshole who told you to stay away. Remember?*"

She was trembling badly, but after a moment, she nodded.

"*I am going to remove my hand. You stay real quiet, OK?*"

Again she nodded. I gently released my fingers from her lips. I was still holding her in a tight embrace so she couldn't move. I whispered, "*How many of them?*"

"*Is this a movie?*"

"*No. How many?*"

"*Four.*"

I knew the guys at the camp must have seen me intercept her, though they would have no idea what that meant or what had happened. If I let Allivya go charging back to the camp, in the state they were in, Dyno was capable of shooting her on sight. I had no choice but to reveal my position.

"*Dyno!*"

His voice came back, "*Yeah! You OK?*"

"*Your friend's coming over.*"

"*...OK.*"

I held her real tight and whispered close in her ear. "*I am going to cover you. You crawl or you crouch. You go as fast as you can, but you do not stand or run. You got that?*" She nodded. I added, "*When I say, not before.*"

"*OK.*"

I let her go and rolled on my belly but kept a hand on her back. I scanned the blackness of the trees and the undergrowth, searching for glimmers of green light. One! For a fraction of a second. A moment later, two flickered close beside the first. I rasped, "*Go! Keep low!*" and double-tapped into the undergrowth, paused for a beat, and triple-tapped half an inch to the right. Again an inch to the left. Behind me, I could hear her stumbling, falling, crying out and whimpering. I peppered the area with twenty shots, keeping them unpredictable but in the general area.

Then I ejected and replaced the extended mag. I glanced behind me. Allivya had been drawn into the circle of the camp. I shouted back at them, "*Keep down!*"

Then I made three, erratic, unpredictable sprints that carried me to the spot where I had been shooting—pretty much the spot from which Allivya had erupted just a while earlier.

I burst from the undergrowth with the Sig held out in front of me. I could see in the eerie, green light, where the branches and foliage and the tree trunks had been ripped and torn by the hail of hot lead. And lying on the ground, with only a very dull green glow, was a guy in black jeans, a black polo sweater, and a black balaclava. His head was lying in a dully glowing pool of green blood.

I hunkered down at the foot of the nearest tree, remained motionless, and brought my breathing to a slow, soft, rhythm. I listened. I listened to every sound, from the rustle of the leaves, the sigh of the breeze and even the crackle of the fire at the camp.

A voice just a couple of feet from me said, "Don't shoot me, I'm just a fuckin' Kiwi. We never hurt anybody."

"Unless you don't like them."

"There is that."

"Did you kill this guy?"

"No, you did. What the fuck are you playin' at, Harry? I've got my bloody work cut out for me keepin' an eye on you, without you bringing fuckin' groupies along."

"I tried to stop them. They wouldn't listen, and the damned crew encouraged them."

"The girl make it?"

"I think so. What about the two guys?"

"Decapitated with very sharp knives. You should bring your TV friends along to have a look. See if they still feel like encouraging groupies."

"I might just do that. Any idea where Del and Gabbai have their camp?"

"Nah, I've been busy babysitting your chums instead of doing my job. I think Del and Gabbai thought all their fuckin' Christmases had come at once when these three showed up. They never stood a chance."

"Rough idea?"

"Yeah, through the forest, where Pine Creek splits. West, Pine Creek spills into Freemont Lake, where you're camped. East you've got Bridger Creek, which then becomes Freemont Creek before it spills into Long Lake—well, just after it splits, you have a big hill west of the creek, where it curls around. For my money, that's where they're holed up."

I visualized the area and nodded. "The girl said there were four of them."

"Six. Five now. I'll try and make it four by tomorrow morning."

It was impossible to say what had changed. There was no sound, and I saw nothing. I had not seen him since he'd spoken to me. But somehow I knew he was no longer there. It was like the air was suddenly empty. I smiled, feeling comforted that he was watching. I had met a number of very dangerous men in my time, but if I had to choose one man I never wanted to have gunning for me, it would have to be the Kiwi. The son of a bitch was lethal.

I made my way silently back to camp, still smiling.

ELEVEN

Back at the camp, they were all gathered around the fire. Dyno and Geoff had rifles, Allivya was curled up sobbing in Chelsea's lap, and Paul and Nestor were in their tent, peering out. I went and sat beside the girls. I pulled the goggles off my head and called to Dyno. I tossed him the goggles as he approached.

"You take the first watch. Lie down on your belly, in the shadows to the left of the fire. Four hours. I'll take the second watch. Geoff, you take the third."

Dyno caught the goggles. As he put them on, Geoff snarled at me, "Who put you in charge?"

I looked him straight in the eye. "Me. Is that something you want to discuss?" He didn't answer. I said, "That's the second time you've given me trouble. Next time I'm going to whip your ass. Is *that* something you want to discuss?" I waited. He still didn't answer. "You've gone awful quiet, Geoff. Sit down."

He sat. I said, "Can everybody hear me?" Dyno said he could, and so did Paul and Nestor from their tent. "There are five men out there who want to kill me. There were six, but I just killed one of them. For reasons I won't go into, they are not just willing to kill the people around me, they are positively happy to do so. So those boys you"—I turned and looked hard at Chelsea—"and you were so willing to encourage to come along with us, when I warned you not to, those boys are now dead."

Allivya curled in tighter into the fetus position and clung to Chelsea. Chelsea gave me a look that was reproachful, and I snarled at her.

"Don't even dream about it. This morning this was a possibility I tried to avoid. Now it's a reality we have to face. And that is because of you. So here is how this is going to go down."

Geoff drew breath. I looked him in the eye. He licked his lips and closed his mouth. I went on.

"We survive the night." I raised a finger. "That is the first and most important part of the plan. We do that by pulling together, by supporting and helping each other. Nobody in this group has a tenth of the experience I have in this kind of situation. So you accept my authority and do as I say without question. Discord and conflict lead very quickly to death." I pulled my Sig and aimed it straight at Geoff's head. "If you give me trouble, if you create discord or conflict, I will shoot you dead on the spot. You will not put the rest of us at risk. Look at my hand."

His eyes were wide, sweat had broken out on his forehead, and he stared at the weapon. I went on.

"I just killed a man ten minutes ago. Do you see my hand shaking or wavering?" He shook his head. His breathing had accelerated, and he grunted involuntarily. I said, "Look into my eyes, Geoff. Do you see doubt or hesitation? If I need to shoot you so the rest of us can survive the night, I will do it without hesitation. Have you understood that clearly?"

His voice was a croak. "Yes."

Dyno's voice came to me from over on my left. "Stop pointing the gun at him, man."

"Go back to your post, Dyno. They might come back, and we are depending on you to spot them."

There was a rustle, and I knew he had done as I'd said. Geoff swallowed hard and said, "I've pissed my pants. Can I go and change?"

I put the Sig back in my holster. "Don't give me any more trouble, Geoff." He moved to his tent, and I continued talking. "Tomorrow as soon as the sun rises, you will go back to the parking lot, get in your vehicles, and go home—"

Chelsea sat erect and scowled at me. "What are you going to do?"

"I'm going to engage them so that you have the chance to get away."

"That was *not* the deal! What about the series? What about Dave? What about the show?"

"People are dying, Chelsea!"

"OK! It was stupid of me to encourage these kids to follow us. I didn't realize then how serious it was—"

"The clue was in Dave getting blown in half!" I said savagely.

"*I'm sorry!* But let Geoff take Allivya—"

Nestor cut in. "I go too. Danger money or no, I did not expect this."

She turned to the director. "Paul? You'll stay, right? You and Dyno can take care of camera and sound. We *can't* let this go. On tonight's footage alone, the ratings will be through the roof!"

I scowled at her, and then at Paul. "You *filmed* what happened tonight?"

Paul shrugged. "Of course, Harry. It's what we do. Other people eat and drink and breathe. We film."

"What are you going to do?" It was Chelsea with a bitter twist in her voice. "Shoot us all?"

"I won't need to," I snarled. "You're going to get yourselves killed without any help from me." I pointed out into the darkness. "There are five professional assassins out there, men trained by the Taliban who have actively engaged in rape, murder, and the massacre of women and children. They want me dead, but more than that, they want to punish me by torturing and killing the people around me. That's you. You need to go! You need to leave at first light while I go and find these men and kill them." There was silence. I raised my voice slightly. "Dyno, will you talk some sense into your producer?"

His voice came back with a hint of a smile in it. "Nope. No can do, Harry. I hear you, and I respect what you're saying. But a film crew like us can wait a whole lifetime and not get a chance like this. Like the lady said, unless you shoot us all, which would be kind of self-defeating, some of us are staying to make this movie."

Geoff emerged from his tent wearing a new pair of pants.

"Me and Nestor will take the girl back in the morning. This is too damn rich for my blood."

"Good." I turned to Chelsea. "And you had better get it into your head. I do not want you here tomorrow."

She met my eye, and her jaw set like quick-drying cement. "Tough shit, big guy. You have your job, we have ours. Suck it up!"

I addressed them all. "Stay out of sight. Get in your tents and stay low. I'll be coming and going during the night."

I crawled over beside Dyno.

"Change of plan."

"Sorry if we're screwing things up, man. But this is our job, it's what we do."

"I'm going out for a few hours. I'm going to need the goggles. You need to stay awake and focused. It could be a long night, and neither Geoff nor Nestor nor Paul is up to the job. So here's what you're going to do. You build up the fire so it gives you light, but you and everybody else, you stay in the shadows. When I come back, I will let you know I am approaching with a whistle like a northern mockingbird."

"A northern mockingbird?"

"It's the only bird I can imitate."

"What the hell does it sound like?"

I gave him a brief demonstration. He shrugged and said, "OK…"

"You see anyone approach, they don't make that sound and they don't identify themselves, you shoot them."

"Got it. Any point asking how long you're going to be?"

"Sure." I thought about it: a little over three miles there and back, one and a half hours, half an hour to do the job brought it to two hours, plus half an hour for unforeseen eventualities. "Say two or two and a half hours."

"You want me to come with you? I'm a good shot."

I shook my head. "I appreciate it. These people need you to keep them alive."

I spent twenty minutes or half an hour organizing teams to bring abundant firewood to keep the fire burning bright for the next three hours. Then I got them secluded and wrapped up warm, but not in the tents. The tents would be obvious targets for strafing or even fire-bombing. I needed them in the dark, outside the tents; and while they were busy doing all of that, I took Dyno's googles and slipped away into the darkness.

I was familiar with the area from the hunting trips I had done there, and I followed the easiest track, the one Del and Gabbai would be most likely to follow in the opposite direction, to arrive at our camp for a surprise lightning strike. I reasoned it would be unlikely they would take a circuitous route in that wilderness if the imperative was speed and surprise. So I took the path that would lead me to intercept them.

It was not easy terrain. There were no tracks here, so it was hard to get a rhythm. Every step was different. Now it was loose rocks, then next step some shrubs, then a fallen tree or a branch, a pothole or a small stream.

All you could do was focus and make a rhythm out of how you timed each step. I took ten steps walking and then ten steps at a trot. Then ten walking and another ten at a trot, all the while keeping my five senses alert for any sign of approaching bodies.

It was cold, and I wore my blanket as a cloak with a

woolen scarf around my mouth to conceal the plumes of condensation that issued on my breath. There was no moon, and the tall trees obscured much of the sky, filtering out the starlight. In such conditions, silent progress was impossible, especially as speed was of the essence. The best I could do was try to ensure that what noises I made were irregular and did not convey purpose or direction. That's not so hard when you have the luxury of moving slowly. But when you need to move fast, concealing direction and purpose is hard.

The first mile was through dense pinewoods, and I headed for one of two small, marshy lakes that separate Freemont from Long Lake. It's easy to get lost in a forest. It is one hundred percent easier at night. But I knew that keeping the black body of water on my right would lead me in an ark to the hill where the Kiwi had told me he thought Del and Gabbai were camped with their men.

The last five hundred yards were a steady ascent up a steep hill that rose sudden and stark between Pine Creek on west and Freemont Creek on the eastern side. It was densely forested in some areas, but on others, particularly toward the top, it was bare but for the thick covering of sagebrush.

At about a hundred and fifty yards, I saw the first sign that they were there: a glimmer of green firelight through the sparse, black silhouettes of the pine trees. Now I slowed. Now progress would be arrhythmic, sporadic, with protracted periods of immobility followed by sudden move-ment forward, to the left, or to the right. Most of the progress, especially over the last two hundred yards, would be at a crouching run or, increasingly, at a crawl.

At sixty yards, I lay on my belly under the vast sweep of the Milky Way, under the black dome of the sky, and watched the flickering green light of their fire, and the unreal, spectral figures of the men who moved about the camp. My fear that they would return that night for a surprise strike on our camp had obviously been unfounded. Either they planned to take their time because they believed us to be outgunned and outmanned, or I had hurt them more than I thought when I took out the guy who was after Allivya, and right now they were licking their wounds.

As I lay there, I could see one guy sitting, silhouetted against the green flames. He had some kind of assault rifle resting between his crossed legs, but it was impossible to see if he had goggles on or not. One thing was clear: He was making no effort to conceal himself. He didn't look like they were expecting an attack. That didn't surprise me. As far as they were concerned, I was one guy, hampered in my movements by my crew. Some part of my mind I wasn't ready to listen to right then asked, not for the first time, how they had known we were coming, and exactly *where* we were coming. They obviously had surveillance on me, but it was damn good and efficient.

I took five minutes to crawl five yards closer, to the cover of a large black cottonwood tree. Now as well as the lookout with the assault rifle, I could see three men seated around the fire with the intense green light from the fire reflecting off them. I could see the black shapes of a couple of tents and one guy who stood at the entrance to one of those tents. They were not afraid. They still believed themselves to be the hunters.

Very slowly, I rose to a kneeling position behind the tree. From my rucksack, I took the Mongol bow and strung it. I nocked one carbon arrow. At twenty-nine inches, it allowed for a good draw on the bow, and with a four hundred spine it was rigid and its flight was true. It had a razor sharp broadhead which, with sixty pounds of thrust behind it would slice clean through a two hundred and twenty pound man.

There are various techniques for aiming a bow. It's not a simple matter. I favor three fingers below the nock and sighting along the arrow. But you can't do that at night, when distance is distorted by lack of light and moving shadows caused by the fire. Sometimes, shooting a bow has to be intuitive. For that, you have to shoot a lot, until every muscle in your body knows the bow and its forces.

I do that, and I hunt exclusively with a bow. This night, I was the hunter, and the guy standing by the tent was the prey, though he didn't know it. I stood silently, close within the shadow of the tree. I drew to the full twenty-nine inches of the shaft, leaned my head to look along the arrow, and saw, in my mind, that broad razorblade thudding home through his sternum—and I loosed.

The silenced string whispered and took sharp death with it through the trees. I didn't wait for the kill. I drew again and took aim at the guy sitting by the fire. Behind him, I saw the guy standing by the tent sway and begin to sink. The guys sitting beside the fire looked up at him. I loosed, and again, quiet death whispered through the trees. I waited a second to see the shaft slip through his throat, severing his spinal cord. Then I moved back, not too fast, in silence, following an erratic, unpredictable path down the hill toward the lake.

As the black water began to appear through the trees and the ground began to level off, I allowed myself a smile. They had killed two innocent boys who had nothing to do with my crew and far less to do with Ernie, Dave, the Kiwi, and me. In return, I had killed three of their men.

As I reached the muddy shore, I hunkered down. The western horizon was paling with the rising moon. I listened in total silence. There were no sounds of pursuit. I wondered if they had realized yet that they were now the prey, and Harry was the hunter.

TWELVE

When I arrived back at camp, a half-moon was hanging low in a paling sky over the eastern horizon. I whistled like a mockingbird a few times and saw Dyno's head and shoulders pop up out of the bushes to peer into the predawn shadows. I sighed and shook my head as I circled the camp to enter from the lake side. From behind, I saw Dyno up on his knees, in full sight, calling in a stage whisper, "*Harry? Is that you?*"

"Lucky for you it was," I said, and he jumped out of his skin and spun to face me. "*Jesus!*" He half shouted it. "I could have shot you!"

"Unlikely. But get up on your knees like that to peer into the dark, and you may as well paint a target on your chest. OK, let's get everybody awake and packing up. You are all moving out."

It didn't take long, especially for Allivya, Nestor, and Geoff. They had their tent down and packed along with their personal stuff within fifteen minutes. But I noticed that, as I had expected, Chelsea, Paul the director, and Dyno did not pack. Instead, Chelsea stoked the fire and made coffee while Dyno prepared some breakfast.

I sat down with them around the fire while Geoff and Nestor finished packing. I ignored Chelsea and spoke instead to Dyno.

"I killed two of them last night. There are three left. That doesn't make them forty percent less dangerous. These people thrive on self-sacrifice and revenge. They will be more dangerous now than before. I can't see the future, but I can tell you this much: If you stay, you will be dead by tonight. And if I go out there to look for them, to hunt them down and kill them, you cannot come with me, with your cameras and your mikes. Because you will hamper me and put my life at risk. So no prime time footage, no rates-busting images. You're wasting your time. Be smart and go."

The three of them looked at each other in some kind of silent exchange. Then Chelsea said, "No." Straight and simple, Dyno shook his head, and Paul shrugged. "It's our job. You do what you have to do, Harry. We won't get in your way. It is our choice. We do what we have to do, like you."

I thought for a moment about aborting the whole thing but decided it was impossible for two reasons. First of all, I couldn't walk away while the Kiwi was still out there, and aside from that, it was better to face these bastards out here in the wilderness than have them follow me into urban areas where their potential targets and victims multiplied exponentially.

I had tried to dissuade them. That was as much as I

could do, aside from lead Del and Gabbai, and whoever was left on their team, away from the crew.

I turned to Chelsea. "You are putting your team in harm's way." I turned to Dyno. "You will almost certainly be killed."

Chelsea cut in. "You've made your point, Harry. You've got your answer."

I guided them for a little less than half a mile, east through the woods. There was no sign of Del and Gabbai, but that didn't surprise me much. Their preference was always to strike at night, and the events of the previous night would have been a shock to them. So they would be licking heir wounds and reviewing their situation.

There was no sign of the Kiwi, either, but I knew he was there, watching.

At the point where the land began to rise toward the trailhead and the Sacred Rim, I stopped. I gathered them around and told them, "Stay in among the trees. Stay low. You'll notice there's a kind of gully. Follow it. It will take you to the trailhead. Keep a steady pace and keep moving. Go."

They turned and set off, and pretty soon they had disappeared from sight, if not from hearing.

Chelsea and Dyno and Paul were all looking at me like they were expecting something.

"I'm going. You won't be able to keep up with me. You will draw a lot of attention. This is probably your last chance. Take it. Go with them."

I didn't wait for an answer. I turned and walked away from them, going south and east into the forest. My plan was essentially the same as the night before: to intercept Del and Gabbai and whatever man or men they had left as they set out to strike at us.

I climbed for maybe an hour, through sagebrush and sparse woodland. I stayed below the horizon and kept to the densely shrubbed areas where I would leave a minimal trail for Chelsea to follow.

Just after midmorning, I stopped at the top of a hill that to the east overlooked the lake and to the north gave me a good view of where Del and Gabbai had camped the night before.

I lay among the trees and the brush for a good hour observing the place but saw nothing and heard nothing but the birds. I figured their camp was about a quarter of a mile away and set off at a gentle trot through the trees. My plan was simple. If they were there, I would kill them. If they had left, they would have left a trail. So I would follow them and kill them.

Either way, that day they would die.

It was when I had crossed the narrow valley and was climbing the hill toward the camp that I heard the distinctive trill of a mockingbird. It made me stop, drop to my belly, and roll in among some old downed timber and some low bushes. I waited, listening, with the P226 in my hand. For thirty seconds, there was nothing but the sigh of the breeze in the pines and the erratic chatter of the birds.

Then the distinctive trill of the mockingbird again followed by six staccato pips. Then silence for thirty seconds, and the same song repeated. The only person who knew the significance of the mockingbird song were Dyno and the Kiwi. There was no way Dyno had kept up with me and no way he could imitate a mockingbird that accurately. So it was the Kiwi, and if he was sending code instead of talking to me, that meant just one thing. Del and Gabbai were in the neighborhood.

I put my fingers in my mouth and returned the call. Fifteen seconds later, it came back, but this time it was the trill followed by just one pip. That was repeated twice more. He was telling me there was one guy. The Kiwi had seen that I was headed for the camp, and he was telling me there was one man watching it.

I waited five minutes without making a sound, then began to move up the side of the hill using a broken, sporadic rhythm so that any sound I made would sound like the movement of an animal through the undergrowth.

I was less than a hundred yards from the camp when I spotted him. If the Kiwi hadn't alerted me, I might not have. He was in a tree, maybe ten or fifteen feet up, and he was immobile. Beneath him were the two guys I'd shot that night, or what was left of them. The smell of blood would not have taken long to attract the wolves once the fire had burned down and the remaining men had left.

All but one: the one who had concealed himself to wait for me.

I needed the kill to be silent. So I was reluctant to use the Sig, but with the branches and the foliage in the way, I didn't have a clear shot with the bow. Very slowly, a couple of feet at a time, I circled around him to my left, keeping within the cover of the trees, looking for a gap in the foliage where I might get a clear shot. There wasn't one. The closest thing was a sixty-yard shot at a six- or seven-inch section of his right thigh. Even for a skilled archer, it was a difficult shot. From a kneeling position, in woodland at a small target in a tree, it was a difficult shot, but it was all I had, and I had to take it.

I crawled behind a large tree trunk, took off my ruck-sack, and strung my bow. I nocked a carbon arrow with a razor sharp broadhead and took up my position on one knee, close in among the shadows of the tree. I spent a good thirty seconds just staring at the patch of military camou-flage from his pants, visualizing the arrow thudding home dead center.

I drew, locked my left arm, and sighted along the shaft, though the truth is that kind of shot has to be intuitive. You cannot aim with a bow in those conditions. Your body, all your muscles, and your unconscious memory combine to give you the feeling that you are either on target or you're not.

I loosed, and the arrow whispered softly. It wasn't a bad shot, but it wasn't perfect. The shaft brushed a small branch as it reached the target and gave a small jump before hitting its mark. The broad razor tip cut deep into his thigh but hit only muscle instead of penetrating deep into the leg, severing veins and arteries as I had intended. I heard a stifled screech, then a cracking of branches as his body tumbled from where he'd been lying.

By the time he hit the ground, I had nocked another arrow and was advancing on him at a run. The guy was tough, though. He was on his feet with his right leg streaming blood from his wound and an assault rifle in his hands.

The next few seconds passed in slow motion. I knew he wanted to shoot, even if he didn't hit me, to alert his pals that I was there. To me, the imperative was silence. He was maybe twenty paces away, raising the rifle, pointing it at my belly. I had the arrow nocked and drawn. If he had pulled the trigger then, he might have missed. His leg was trembling badly and his hands were unsteady, but he would at least have given the signal. Instead he tried for the kill shot and raised the rifle to his shoulder. I saw the action as in a slowed-down film. I saw his eyes lock on to mine. I loosed the arrow, and I saw the feathers spin. His eyes shifted to the shaft, and for a fraction of a second, he hesitated.

The arrow plunged into his throat and sliced through his vertebrae, severing the spinal cord. His brain was screaming at his finger to pull the trigger, but his finger never got the memo. His eyes glazed, his legs turned to spaghetti, and he fell to the ground.

Feast day for the wolves.

I approached him and removed the rifle from his hands. It was a KLS, standard issue for the Iranian army and the Islamic Revolutionary Guard Corps. He was wearing gloves and a balaclava. I removed it to reveal his face and was surprised to see that he was blond, pale skinned, and blue-eyed. He looked more Swedish than Afghan.

Or Russian.

Two left.

I has assumed it would be Ben-Amini's nephews, Del and Gabbai. Now I wasn't sure. But if it wasn't them, why the stress on revenge? Why target our patrol?

I searched what was left of the camp but found nothing of interest. So I found their tracks, which were not hard to follow, and set off after them, with two thoughts in my mind. The first was that if the tracks were this easy, they wanted me to follow, and the other was that I would have to keep at least one of them alive long enough to interrogate him.

Their tracks trailed down the west side of the steep hill and seemed to head roughly in the direction of our camp but also the route Geoff, Nestor, and Allivya had taken back toward the trailhead. That didn't worry me too much because I was pretty sure that their main plan was to ambush me.

So after a couple of hundred yards, when I was approaching the bottom of the hill and the denser forest that lay between Lake Freemont and Long Lake, I left their track and immersed myself deep in the dappled shadows and the darkness of the forest and followed their track from there, looking and listening ahead for the sounds they would be making moving over the rough terrain, the loose stones, fallen timber, and abundant small bushes.

It didn't take long. After about twenty minutes, I heard the murmur of voices. It was so quiet that, if I hadn't been consciously listening for it, I would not have heard it. But I caught it, a slight murmur on the breeze.

I froze and hunkered down, motionless, listening. It came again, a little longer, two voices. It was impossible to make out what they were saying, but there was no mistake it was two men talking. And by the cadence and the rounded sounds, I knew it was not Arabic.

I moved as fast as I dared, keeping behind the thick tree trunks, scanning the area below. They had not been careful to hide their tracks, and even at this distance, it was easy to see where they had crushed small bushes and broken branches as they went.

The voices grew closer, and now it was easy to make out

that they were speaking some East European language, and pretty soon I saw the two figures, tall and broad-shouldered in dark military fatigues with balaclavas over their heads. One of them hunkered down while the other scanned the woodland around them. The one who was hunkered down was examining a dead body. I don't speak Russian, but from their body language and the tone of their voices, it was clear they were wondering: if they hadn't done it, who the hell had killed this guy?

That was something I wanted to know too. I also wanted to know, if these guys weren't Del and Gabbai—and they clearly weren't—who the hell were they? And why were they seeking revenge on our patrol?

I pulled my bow from the rucksack and nocked an arrow. I drew and aimed a kill shot at the guy who was standing. The simple plan was to kill him and interrogate the guy who was hunkered down. But as I prepared to loose, that guy stood up, and they both moved off out of sight among the shadows and the trees.

I gave them five minutes, then moved down to look at the body. For a second, I felt dizzy, and my head throbbed. It was Dyno. He was lying face down. His mouth was gaping, and his eyes were bulging—and his throat had been cut from ear to ear. He was practically decapitated.

The knife, after being used to cut his throat, had been plunged into his back to secure a long scarf bearing the legend *Intiquaam*. Revenge.

Revenge in Arabic, not Russian.

THIRTEEN

I had the arrow nocked and left it that way as I followed their trail. I could have closed on them and taken them with the Sig, one in the head and one in the knee, and then had a chat, but something was stopping me. I had finished the puzzle; I had only one piece left, but that piece didn't fit.

Why were they Russians? And why were Russians seeking revenge in Arabic?

The only answer I could think of raised more questions than it answered and made me feel sick to my stomach.

We were approaching the spot where I had left Geoff, Nestor, and Allivya. We were maybe half a mile off, and for a while, I had been looking and listening for signs of the crew, asking myself how they had managed to separate Dyno from the rest to kill him—whoever 'they' were.

I had found no sign of them and had decided the time had come to close in and finish these guys off when I heard a shriek through the trees followed by two yells. I hunkered down behind a large black cottonwood with my bow half-drawn. There was a crashing, stumbling rush approaching through the trees, and suddenly Paul was there, with his face twisted and distorted with terror, hurtling toward me. I stood and stepped out in front of him. He reached for me, screaming. I grabbed him by his shirt, and his momentum pushed us both back a couple of steps into the undergrowth. I was shouting into his face, "Paul! Paul! Stop! It's me! What happened?"

He stared into my face with wild eyes. "Chelsea! Chelsea!"

"What about her? Paul! Focus!" I could hear tramping, running boots approaching. I rasped, "Paul! What happened?"

"They're going to kill us all! Chelsea! You have to get Chelsea!"

Over his shoulder, I saw one of the Russians burst out of the trees with a semi-automatic in his hands. I didn't hesitate. I had been expecting him, and I reacted instantly. I stepped right as I drew to avoid Paul and aimed instinctively in one fluid movement. As I loosed the arrow, he fired, and Paul's head exploded, showering me with gore. But the arrow had struck home through his right arm and into his chest.

He was down on his knees, gripping the feathers with his left hand and making noises that should have aroused compassion in me but didn't. I went behind him. The shaft of the arrow and the broad tip were protruding three inches from his back. I kicked him hard so he sprawled on his face. I knelt on him and ripped off his balaclava. His features could have been Caucasian.

I pulled the Fairbairn-Sykes from my boot and placed the razor tip on his jugular.

"You speak English?"

He spoke like it was an effort because of the pain. "Yes."

"Where is your pal?"

He made painful noises, then said, "Fuck you."

I leaned my knee against the arrow tip and pushed. He screamed. "Where is your pal?"

"In cabin!" He began to weep. "In cabin!"

"Mama didn't tell you it could get tough out here? What cabin? Where?" I gave the arrow head another shove. He made a horrible noise in his throat. "Bottom Sacred Rim, there is big hollow. There is shack in there. We call cabin. Please no more. Please."

I screwed up my brow. "You made a cabin? How long have you been here, for Christ's sake?"

His eyes had glazed. I could see a large pool of blood spreading underneath him. He whispered, "Fuck you, Intiquaam..." and he was gone.

I sheathed my knife and followed his tracks back from where he'd come. He'd been charging after Paul and making no effort to hide his tracks, so they were not hard to follow. After maybe five minutes, the track turned sharp left, west toward Long Lake, at the base of the Sacred Rim. The forest became more dense, and where to my left the grown leveled off toward the lake, on my right, it rose steeply into sharp cliffs. And here, for the first time since we had come down from the trailhead, I saw a clear path made from regular use. In a place like that wilderness, it takes regular use to make a path and keep it from becoming overgrown. These guys had been settled here on some kind of a permanent basis.

And the question kept nagging at me. Why?

Revenge. An eye for an eye. Intiquaam.

But I no longer lived here. I was back in New York. And in any case, it was too much: too much effort, too extravagant, too complicated for a target that was just one man.

Which meant the target had to be bigger, and based in Wyoming.

I stopped. I had covered maybe a mile, and the path had led me to a steep rubble slope that descended to the banks of the lake. Here the trees and bushes stopped, and there was just dirt and rocks. I settled down at the base of a tree and scanned the area. Above me was the sheer cliff face with pine trees and other bushes growing out of the rocks at crazy angles. Ahead, maybe a hundred yards across the slide of rubble and dirt, the woodland continued, but there was no way to cross without sliding down another four hundred yards to the water's edge.

That made me examine the slide more carefully, and sure enough, you could just make out a track where people had repeatedly slid and scampered their way down. It left open the question of how they got back up again, but I had a hunch I could figure that out.

I eased myself onto the slope, which I figured at some point in its history had been an avalanche or rock-fall of some sort, and began to ease myself gently down, following the vague path I could barely make out.

If there was anybody down there, any hope of surprising them was gone. As I moved down, rocks, small boulders, and dirt tumbled down the near-vertical slope before me. More than once, I was certain I was about to go myself, but I kept myself as flat against the face of the slope as I could and bit by bit inched my way down until the slope began to ease off and became a dirty, rubble beach. I found the shelter of a couple of large boulders, hunkered down, and waited while I scanned the area for the opening to a cave.

It didn't take me long to find it. It was on the far side of the landslide, maybe a hundred yards up from the edge of the water, where a rocky outcrop jutted from the face of the cliff. Two massive rocks leaned in on each other, forming a gap at the base maybe fifteen or twenty feet across. From it you could just make out a narrow, beaten track to the shore of the lake.

The loosened rocks and dirt I had sent down ahead of me did not seem to have alerted anybody, so after another ten minutes, I scrambled across and followed the track to the strangely temple-like entrance. There I flattened myself against the cliff wall and waited again, listening, scanning the area around me. Again, there was nothing. So I got down on my belly and peered around into the darkness. For a second, I saw nothing but blackness. Nobody shot me, but I withdrew my head anyhow and lay for a minute and a half with my eyes closed, listening for sounds inside.

After I had counted to ninety with my eyes shut, I peered in again. Though a wedge of glare cut across the darkness, making the shadows deeper, after having had my eyes closed, I could now see more clearly. And what I could see was, maybe twenty feet away, rock and stone covered in lichen and after a moment, as I grew accustomed to the shadows, a narrow hole in the rock face, maybe seven feet across and eight feet tall. That was the true entrance to the cave. I slipped in and ran quietly to the opening. There I flattened myself against the wall and again listened. But all I heard was silence. Deep, still silence.

I held the Sig out in front of me and moved through the doorway one slow step at a time. I was expecting darkness, and for the first twenty or thirty feet, what I saw was a cavern, some fifteen feet across and maybe twenty or thirty feet high, littered with rocks and boulders, all in deep shadows. But where the cavern curved gently to the left, at the end, there was a long gash in the wall, and through that gash came the flickering, amber glow of firelight.

I moved through the darkened cavern, scanning the rocks and boulders for an ambush but keeping my hearing focused on the flickering gap. Still there were no voices, no sounds at all.

When I got there, it was more than just a gash. The angle from which I had seen it made it look narrow, but it was a good ten or twelve feet across and easily fifteen feet high. The wall beyond it was bathed in firelight, and now I could hear the crackle and spark of burning wood. I got down on one knee and peered into the next cavern. It was surreal.

The cavern itself was huge. The ceiling was lost in shadows but was at least a hundred and fifty feet high. At its widest point, it must have been eighty to ninety feet across. In depth it was hard to say. The floor of the cave was pretty flat, as though it had been cleared, but eighty to a hundred yards in, the cave narrowed from the right, curled around, and continued on into the mountain.

And right there, where it narrowed, there was a log cabin. Just like a log cabin you might find anywhere in the west, on a prairie or in the mountains, with its windows and its chimney and its decking. Over to my right, halfway between where I stood at the entrance to the cavern and the cabin, there was a large fire burning small tree trunks and hefty branches, illuminating the cavern and casting flickering reflections on the glass in the cabin windows.

The door to the cabin opened, and a man stepped out. He was in military fatigues with a cap on his head, but it was hard to make out his face at this distance. He gestured to me to come closer and called out so his voice echoed up in the darkness.

"I have a man with a bead on you right now. You might as well put away the Sig."

I lowered it but kept it in my hand as I approached the cabin. There were two chairs set on the deck on either side of a table. He sat.

"It's the bears," he said as I drew closer. "They come in, in the winter, sleepy and bad-tempered. We don't like to kill them if we can avoid it. So we have the cabin."

At twenty yards, I could see he was probably an Afghan, though his English was educated and suggested a private school and university. I said, "Where's Chelsea?"

"Inside."

"Who are you?"

"The man who is going to kill you."

I had the Sig leveled at his right knee when the cabin door opened. There was a guy there. By his shape and size, I figured he was the other Russian. He had his left arm around Chelsea's neck and what looked like an MP-443 Grach semi-automatic aimed at the side of her head.

The guy in the chair smiled and pointed behind me. I looked over my shoulder, and there was a man in fatigues aiming a rifle at me. The guy in the chair laughed.

"I wonder if you have ever been this close to death."

"Sure," I said. "When I killed your uncle. Which one are you, Del or Gabbai?"

"Put your gun on the ground, along with your rucksack and your knife, then come up here on the deck."

I dropped the pistol and the rucksack and pulled the hunting knife from my belt. Then I climbed the steps. I paused to look into Chelsea's terrified face. "Dyno is dead. So is Paul. Nobody to get it all on film. I told you to leave. Next time I tell you to do something, do it."

I watched her face twitch and her brow clench, but there were no tears in her eyes.

I turned to the man in the chair. He was watching me like he was amused.

"I am Gabbai," he said and gestured to the chair across the table from his. "Sit, Mr. Bauer." He looked at the man who was holding Chelsea. "Take her down. Put her on her knees. When I tell you, shoot her in the head."

Chelsea began to scream and beg. The big Russian dragged her down and forced her to her knees. Gabbai returned his gaze to me and said more firmly, "Sit."

I sat. He said, "I have a lot of questions for you. Normally a man of your strength would not answer my questions, even under torture." He gave a disdainful laugh. "Far less under threat of death. A man like you accepts death, even embraces it." He paused and shrugged. "Unless of course it is somebody else's death."

He stood and took a couple of steps to the edge of the deck, where he gazed down at Chelsea. She was staring at me. Her mouth was twisted, and her cheeks were wet with tears. Her eyes were begging for me to do something.

"What is worse, do you think, Harry?" He turned to look at me. "Death, or suffering?" I didn't say anything, and he went on. "I find people who have a firm belief in some kind of afterlife are less concerned with death and worry more about pain and suffering. Do you believe in an afterlife, Harry?"

"What do you want, Gabbai?"

He frowned. "I want to know if you believe in an afterlife. To us, that is a very important part of what makes a good soldier."

I sighed. "I never really thought about it."

He laughed out loud. "A man who has killed as much as you have, and you never thought about what comes after death?"

A sudden surge in irritation made me raise my voice. "Yes! OK, Gabbai, I think probably there is a life after death. Now what?"

"So"—he pointed down at Chelsea—"if he puts a bullet through her head, that will upset you, but you can seek solace in the fact that she has gone to another life, possibly a better one. But if he cuts off her fingers, her cheeks, subjects her to days of cruel suffering. That would be something you could not live with."

"I already asked you what you want. You're overselling your product. Tell me what you want. I'll give it to you. But let her go."

He chuckled. "Oh, Harry, you don't make conditions. You do as you're told, and you hope for the best."

"So again, what do you want?"

"Who do you work for?"

"Wrong question, Gabbai. I resigned a few months ago. I

worked for an organization that assassinates high profile targets."

"After you left the SAS?"

"We had your uncle. The CIA came and took him from us and gave him a safe house in California. I was approached by this organization and offered the job of tracking him down and taking him out. I accepted.[1]"

His eyes were bright, and he was smiling. He pulled off his cap and ran his hand over his crewcut. "You are actually telling the truth. I am surprised."

"Sure I am. I play ball, you let her go. The moment I start to believe you won't let her go, it makes no difference whether I play ball or not. So I stop playing ball. It's simple."

He sat. "What is the name of the organization?"

I spoke without thinking. "It goes by the acronym JBL. It stands for Justice Beyond the Law. The idea was we took out people who had committed crimes against humanity but whom the law could not reach."

"Like Netenyahu?"

"More like Osama bin Laden and Mohammed Ben-Amini, your uncle."

His face darkened. "You do not do yourself favors with that kind of talk, Harry."

"I was always more of a wiseass than just plain wise."

"So you were employed to assassinate the enemies of the West. Who is at the head of this agency? Be very careful how you answer this question."

"If you already know the answer, what's the point in asking?"

---

1. See *Dead of Night*

He sat down again with his elbows on his knees and looked into my face. "I don't know the answer, Harry, but I suspect it. And if you give me an answer which I know to be false, I will have Sergei put three 9 mm rounds through Chelsea's right knee. The best that will happen to her is that she will lose the leg. The worst is that she will die a slow, painful death from gangrene. Who is the head of JBL?"

I was in a corner, and he knew it. I had a hunch Chelsea was too valuable for him to cause her serious harm—but that was just a hunch. I took a deep breath and said, "My CO when I was in the Regiment..."

I trailed off. The muscles in my throat and mouth wouldn't articulate his name. Gabbai smiled.

"It is what I suspected. Your director is Brigadier Alexander 'Buddy' Byrd!"

FOURTEEN

HE PULLED A PACK OF CIGARETTES FROM HIS pocket. Shook one free and poked it in his mouth straight from the pack. He lit it with a red, plastic disposable lighter and squinted at me through the smoke.

"He trained you, selected you, and after you tried my uncle at a kangaroo court in the desert and tried to execute him against the rules of the Geneva Convention, he inducted you into his organization to track down a legitimate refugee and murder him."

"You're forgetting something, Gabbai. I witnessed with my own eyes what your legitimate refugee did to the people in that village. There is a face—the face of a four-year-old girl —that will haunt me till the day I die."

He shrugged, and his mouth pulled down at the corners. "They were infidels. In the Koran, it says, 'You will increase your hatefulness in the eyes of Allah, disbeliever, for you are one of the worst living creatures. Verily, the worst living creatures before Allah are those who disbelieve.' That is the eighth chapter." He leaned forward and pointed at me. "The Koran says, 'If you could see when the angels take away the souls of those who disbelieve, they smite their faces and their backs, saying: "Taste the punishment of the blazing Fire."' It says, 'Do you know what you will drink in Hell? Those who disbelieve will drink boiling water, and the angels will laugh to watch them.'" He raised the finger he had been pointing. "'Surely, those who disbelieve our signs We shall burn them in fire, and as often as their skin is roasted through, we shall give them new skins that they may taste the punishment. Truly Allah is most powerful and wise. Neither will the fire have a complete killing effect on them so that they die, nor shall its torment be lightened. Thus do We requite every disbeliever.'"

"She was a child of four."

"This is not an argument you can win. God has spoken. You must obey. The director of JBL is Brigadier Alexander 'Buddy' Byrd, correct?"

I nodded and knew as I did so that this man had to die. "Yes," I said. "That's him."

"Then I have good news for you. A chance to save your life, and hers."

He stood and threw back his head and laughed. I caught Chelsea's eye. She was staring at me, and there was terror in her face. Gabbai stopped laughing and smiled down at me.

"We also created a league of assassins. We modeled it on the old Persian Hashishim."

"But you called it Intiquaam."

He shook his head and picked a piece of tobacco from

his lip. "That is not the name. It is our battle cry, if you like. My brother thought of it. Because he wanted to avenge our uncle. Then we thought we would avenge the whole Arabic nation for the injustices perpetrated by the West and the Jews. We called it aldam bialdam." He held my eye a moment, smiling through the smoke. "It means blood for blood. It means for every drop of blood an Arab spills, we will empty a Western body or a Jewish body. I told you I have good news for you."

"I doubt it."

He ignored my comment and went on. "A chance to save Chelsea's life and your own."

"Yeah? By doing what?"

"First you convert to Islam, publicly." He waved his hand at Chelsea. "I don't care about her. She can convert, and if she doesn't, you can have her. But you convert and make a public display, ex-SAS soldier, a Christian, converts to Islam, And then, Harry, you kill the brigadier. Kill Alexander 'Buddy' Byrd."

I stared at him a long time. He would expect me to struggle, and he'd be suspicious if I didn't. I switched my gaze to Chelsea. Her bottom lip was trembling. I snarled, "Tell that baboon to take that goddamn gun away from her head."

He hesitated a moment, then snapped something at the guy, who holstered his gun. Chelsea closed her eyes, sagged, and her breath shuddered. I turned to Gabbai.

"I will make a public show of converting to Islam, but that's all it would be. I am not religious, and much as I might want to, I cannot be a true believer."

He shrugged. "That will come in time. We will take care

of you. You will grow to love Islam, as we all do. And when you kill the brigadier, you will make the commitment. There will be no turning back then."

I sighed and rubbed my face. "I can do a deal with you. I have a lot of information—"

"No! The deal is as I have said it. There is no other deal. That is it." He snapped something at Sergei, and the big Russian pulled his gun. I half got to my feet, holding out my hands toward him, saying, "No, no, no! Wait! OK. Take it easy. I'm on board. How do we do this?"

He pointed at Chelsea. "You want her?"

"Yes, goddammit! Just don't hurt her!"

He smiled. "The Lord is merciful and the Lord is great. You want her, you can have her." He turned to Chelsea. "Go to him. He is your master now."

She scrambled away from Sergei, and I got to my feet as she ran onto the deck and took her in my arms. I held her tightly and spoke softly in her ear. "Why the hell didn't you listen to me, Chelsea? I warned you how dangerous this could be!"

She clung tightly and sobbed into my chest. Gabbai said, "Sit down, Harry. We are a long way from a place where I will trust you standing up." I sat back in my chair, and he addressed Chelsea. "Sit at his feet. From now on you will serve him. Do you understand?"

She nodded. "Yes."

To me, he said, "You see how quickly things can change when you serve God faithfully?"

"Yeah, sure. Now you want to tell me how we are going to do this? You send me off to DC to take care of Buddy, and meanwhile you hang on to Chelsea, and how do I know you won't be raping her, abusing her, or even killing her?"

He laughed and shook his head. "Well, in the first place, we would not do that to a fellow jihadist, and that is what you will be by tomorrow morning. She is your property, and we will respect that in the name of Allah." He laughed again. "And in the second place, she will go with you. A happy couple, brought together during your work on your documentary."

I narrowed my eyes at him. "That makes no sense at all. It begs the same question, but in reverse. How can you know we won't just disappear—alert Buddy and go AWOL?"

"No, Harry. We will have a team watching you and listening to you at every moment. One step out of line and we will take Chelsea and do things to her that you cannot begin to imagine in your worst nightmares. Sometimes you will see us. Sometimes you will not. But we will always be there." He smiled and gestured at Sergei. "You have seen that we of the aldam bialdam are not necessarily Arabs, though we are all Islamic, and we are all jihadists. We are recruiting widely and training these elite killers to the highest level. They will be watching you and listening to you at every moment."

Chelsea had her head on my knee and was clinging to my leg. I eyed Gabbai. He looked smug.

"If they are so damned good, why don't you send them to kill Buddy?"

"Oh, Harry!" He laughed. "You disappoint me. Think of the coup! When we have safely extracted you and we reveal to the public media that you have killed your brigadier for jihad..." He shook his head. "That has no price. That will be a triumph for us."

I grunted. "Where is Del?"

He frowned. "Why do you ask that?"

"Was this his idea?"

"Partly. We discussed it."

"But he's not here. Where is he? In Afghanistan?"

His mouth said, "That is none of your concern," but his face had already told me his brother was still in Afghanistan. I told him, "We are tired and hungry. If we are going to do this, we need some rest and some food."

"Of course you do. You'll find inside is a little bigger than you might expect. Your room is at the end of the passage, on the right."

I stood and pushed through the door. The cabin, such as it was, had been constructed onto the rock face, covering the entrance to a smaller—though still large—cave. This had been exploited and worked on to provide spacious and comfortable accommodation for at least six people.

I turned and frowned at him. "How long have you been here?"

"Oh, hard to answer that, Harry. Strictly, ten years give or take. But actually, since a little before nine-eleven."

I screwed up my brow and shook my head. "*Why?* What possible interest could the Winds have for Islam?"

He threw back his head and laughed out loud. "You mean besides being the remotest place in the USA and having Billionaire Central just up the road in Jackson?" He took a step toward me so he was barely a foot away. "Do you know what I can offer, in terms of oil-related benefits, to a man with a hundred million dollars to spare? But if I approach that man in New York, Los Angeles, Washington, DC, or Houston, he will shy away from me. He will not want to be associated with me. But if I meet him in the Cowboy Bar in Jackson Hole, who the hell is going to know? Who the hell is going to care? Hey! He might even invite me to his thousand acre ranch at the foot of the Tetons, and nobody would ever know."

He threw back his head again and laughed. "This is an invasion, Harry. You just want to make sure you are on the winning side. Most of your political class have already switched. It's just a matter of time."

I stared at him, and the shadows began to evaporate in my mind.

"But of course, where you find still the most resistance is in the military. They have other values. So you need some subtle weapon to deliver deadly poison into the military body. Destroy their moral, their belief in themselves..."

He smiled the kind of smile that you don't want to see in a dark alley at night and nodded. "While your sick, corrupted politicians do their best to divide and poison the national identity, you will lead the campaign to poison the military identity. An exquisite revenge, don't you think, Harry? I don't kill you. I take possession of you and make you kill what you must love." His smile deepened. "So now you understand, will you go ahead and do it? Or"—he pointed at Chelsea—"shall I start to take off her limbs with a blunt razorblade?"

I growled, "I told you I'd do it. Leave her alone."

"Yes, of course, Harry. You will take each painful step toward your perdition, believing passionately all the way that at the next step you will be able to break free, take some heroic leap—with one bound our hero is free! But it is already too late, Harry." He came a step closer. "You already belong to me."

I held his gaze and spoke quietly. "Take it easy, Gabbai. I said I'll do it, and I will. But for that kind of job, if you want the best from me, I am going to need a lot more than this woman. You'd better break open your piggy bank, pal." I went to step into the bizarre cabin-cum-cave but stopped and looked back at him. "And, Gabbai? If I have given my word to become a Muslim, join your jihad, and poison the American military, none of that is a guarantee that I won't come after you. I don't belong to you, Gabbai, but I might just kill you."

I stepped inside and heard the door slam behind me. We were in a large room with a wooden floor. To the left, there was a large wooden table with half a dozen chairs. To the right was a sitting area with a couple of sofas and several armchairs. There was also a TV, a couple of bookcases, and a tray of drinks. Real civilized.

The door opened, and the guy who'd held a gun to Chelsea's head came in. He ignored us, walked to the sofa, and switched on the TV.

There was a passage at the back of the room. We moved down it and found the door at the end on the right was open. The room was large, with a large bed and an en suite bathroom and shower. There were no windows. I stepped through and heard Chelsea slam the door behind me. She rushed to me and grabbed my arm.

"Harry, what are you doing? You can't go ahead with this."

"No? What should I do? Let them cut you to pieces?

Sometimes life sucks and you have to do things you don't want to do. And watch what you say. This place is probably bugged."

She pressed close to me, and I held her arms, pulling her closer. She spoke in a raw whisper.

"Harry, we have to escape! Who is the brigadier? Is he a friend? You can't kill him. We have to warn him—"

"Stop! I am not going to let them hurt you. I have made a commitment, and I will see it through. You heard what he said. They will be watching us—and listening to us—every step of the way."

She shook her head. Her face was twisted like she was going to start crying.

"But out there, you seemed indestructible. The things you did—"

"I did because I am a realist. I don't deal in dreams or fantasies, Chelsea. I have one immediate problem. If I don't do what they demand, they will torture you and kill you. I can't let that happen. Do I have to kill the brigadier? Do I have to kill other senior Western officers and poison the military system? OK, soldiers sign up to get killed. It's what we do: We kill and we get killed. And if the system is so weak and corrupt that one man can bring it down by destroying the moral and the system's belief in itself, then maybe it's time for that system to fail and be replaced."

She shook her head. "I can't believe you are talking like this."

"Can you believe reality? Because that is what I am talking about. Get real, Chelsea."

"What are you going to do...?" Her voice was almost a whisper.

"What am I going to do? I am going to take you to New York as my fiancée. I am going to arrange a meeting with the brigadier and inform him that we managed to kill the Intiquaam sect and avenge Ernie and Dave. I am going to arrange dinner with him at my place in New York to introduce him to my beautiful, film producer fiancée. Then I am going to send you out to get ice from the corner store, and I am going to kill the brigadier. His life for yours."

FIFTEEN

She backed away a couple of steps and sat on the bed, staring at me.

"You'd do that for *me?*" She gave her head a small shake. "*Why?*"

I went to the bathroom door, stripping off my shirt. I turned back and pointed at her.

"And I'll take photographs, and I'll send them to Gabbai as proof of what I've done. Hell! I'll take him his head if he wants it. And then I'm going to demand ten million dollars payment for the job."

She was shaking her head as I spoke. When I'd finished, she said, "Harry, no! I don't like hearing you talk like this. Why? Why would you do this?"

I scrunched up my shirt and threw it on the bed.

"First," I said, "because I have no choice."

"You have!" She stood and came to me again, gripping my arms. "There are five or six men here, no more. You, with your skills, you could escape. You could get out of here!"

I watched her face, staring hard into her eyes. When I spoke, my voice was a thick rasp.

"And what about you? You think I could leave you to these butchers, knowing what they would do to you?"

"But Harry, I don't understand..."

"You don't need to understand. It's enough that you know I wouldn't leave you here. I'll do whatever I have to do, but I won't leave you for them."

I walked to the bathroom again, and again I stopped at the door. I spoke without looking at her. "It was in Helmand Province, in Afghanistan. I watched a whole village massacred by Gabbai's uncle, Mohammed Ben-Amini. There was a girl, a child, barely four or five years old. Her face, the fear in those innocent eyes. It's a nightmare that will never leave me. I won't let that happen to you."

She came up behind me. I felt her cool hand on my back.

"Harry, what happened, with us... I really like you. I am really fond of you, but you do understand. With everything that's happened, I can't—"

I snarled, "That's not what this is about. Forget it."

Her face creased up, and her lower lip curled. "Please don't be hard on me. I am so frightened and confused."

I drew her to me and kissed her savagely, and I ripped off her clothes and threw her on the bed.

An hour later, I left her sleeping and climbed in the shower. I gave it two hot blasts and three cold. Then I pulled on my jeans and my boots, slung a shirt over the top, and went to look for Gabbai.

I found him sitting at the table going through a folder of papers. The big Russian guy was still watching TV. I pulled out a chair and sat.

"I want to meet Del in New York before I execute the brigadier."

"Still making demands?"

"It's not a demand. If I am going to do this, I need to know it's going to work."

"All you need to know, Harry, is that Allah is with you, and if you fail, Chelsea will reach hell days before she dies."

"Wrong. That's how you operate. I was not trained that way, and I don't work that way. I will do this, I'll send you his fucking head by UPS if you want, but I need to know my plan is going to work."

And how will meeting Del in New York help?"

I held up two fingers. "In two ways. First, I want him to arrange the extraction, and I want him to be part of the extraction. That way I know it will be for real and I am not going to be left stranded. Second, I want to look him in the eye and tell him what I am about to tell you: I want ten million dollars in my numbered account in Panama, and I want a full change of identity for me and Chelsea, and a beachside house in Belize. And I don't mean some shack. I mean five bedrooms, a pool, gardens—the works. In exchange for that, I will arrange dinner and a meeting with the brigadier, and I'll tell him to bring along Army General John Moorcroft of the Joint Chiefs of Staff, General Schwarz of the Marines and personal advisor to the president, and Admiral Sam Benner, also advisor to the president. I'll tell him I have an important briefing for them as a result of this job. And I will kill all four of them. Del picks me and Chelsea up, and we disappear."

He gave an amused snort and leaned back in his chair. "What makes you think—"

"Those are my terms. Take it or leave it." Before he could answer, I raised a finger. "And one more thing. You call him now, in my presence, and you make the arrangement. After that, it is radio silence until after the job. We do this my way or no way at all."

He closed his eyes and took a deep breath, like he was counting to ten and wanted me to know it.

"Harry Bauer, you are a supreme pain in the ass."

"Tell me something I don't know."

He gestured at the chair opposite him. "Sit down. I will consult with my brother and see what he says."

I pulled out the chair and sat. "You consult with your brother in English, and we will see what he says."

He made the call, put it on speaker, and got an almost instantaneous response in Arabic, to which he replied, "My brother, I speak to you in English because I have here our friend and brother Harry Bauer."

There was a protracted silence. Then, "You call him a friend and a brother, Gabbai?"

"Oh, I have news for you, Del. Joyful news. Harry has agreed to convert to Islam and join jihad, and to prove his true commitment to the one true god, he has agreed to kill Brigadier Alexander 'Buddy' Byrd."

"Allahu Akbar! That is truly joyful news."

Gabbai began to laugh. "But, my brother, Harry is not any warrior. Harry is a great warrior! And like a true warrior, he must do things his way, and he demands rewards."

"What rewards? If he is a true jihadist, his rewards will come in heaven."

"Hear me out, brother Del. Harry demands ten million dollars transferred into his account in Panama. He wants a complete change of identity for him and for Chelsea, who is a television producer and has become his great love, and a fine beachside house in Belize where they can retire."

I could hear Del laughing on the other end of the phone. "Tell him—" He paused to laugh some more. "Tell him, my brother, I want all this also!"

They both laughed for a bit, and Gabbai repeated several times, like it was a hilarious punch line to a joke, "Me also! Me also, brother!"

When he got around to wiping the tears from his eyes, he said, "But you know, my brother Del, I would not have called you if there was not more. Harry, who is a great warrior, now inspired by his love for Chelsea and his new faith in Islam, promises in return this: He will arrange a dinner for the brigadier and also Army General John Moorcroft, of the Joint Chiefs of Staff, General Schwarz of the Marines, personal advisor to the president, and Admiral Sam Benner, also advisor to the president. He will give us their heads. Their deaths will be announced to the press as the work of American soldier Harry Bauer, trained for eight years by the British SAS." He glanced at me and added, "And after this job, if we give him a safe home and a new identity, he will still be available for other jobs, correct, Harry?"

I nodded. "Sure." I pointed at him. "And the extraction."

"He wants to meet you in New York, and after the job, he wants you personally to perform the extraction for him and Chelsea."

There was another protracted silence. Then, "British Brigadier Alexander Byrd, American Army General John Moorcroft, Joint Chiefs of Staff, General Schwarz, he is of the Marine Corps and also personal advisor to the president, and Admiral Sam Benner, also advisor to the president. And he will give us their heads."

"Yes, brother, and then we can tell the world that SAS Sergeant Harry Bauer, an American, has joined Islamic Jihad and killed these generals and this admiral."

"For this he wants a new identity for him and his woman, a house on the beach in Belize—"

"Five bedrooms and a swimming pool."

"And ten million dollars."

"Yes, brother."

A shorter silence, then "Yes, brother. I think this is good. I will go to New York. I also want to see him. In two days we meet. We will go to the apartment. I need his contact number. He comes to see me, and he brings his woman."

"Very good, Brother Del, your decision is always wise. I am sending you his number. Allahu Akbar!"

"Allahu Akbar!"

He hung up, looked at me, and spread his hands. "Harry Bauer, a man who always gets what he wants. Maybe you are beloved of Allah, and he is trying to save your soul."

"Yeah," I said without trying to hide the irony in my voice. "That's what I thought." I screwed up my eyes and gave my head a shake that suggested incredulity. "You've had this place for over twenty years?"

He nodded.

"And how many men have you got here? Six, eight?" He looked uncomfortable. I raised both hands. "I am not prying. I am just curious. Because, Gabbai, I have to tell you, our standard patrol is four guys, and in a week or two, we can do a lot of damage. If four of our guys had a hideout like this, and twenty years, we'd have brought the country down by now. Have you got a factory here? You make bombs?"

"That's a lot of questions, Harry."

"Yeah? I thought we were brothers in Allah now. I am just questioning your efficiency. You know the Regiment is probably the most efficient fighting force on the planet. We do maximum damage with minimum effort. But you, with this incredible operational headquarters at your disposal, I-80 just down the road to take you to New York or California, I-15 to take you south. Man, the damage we could do with a setup like this." He frowned. I pressed him. "Seriously, how many guys can you fit in this place?"

He shrugged. "At a push, maybe fifteen men."

I gave a bark of a laugh. "Three patrols and three controllers. You could hit New York, Los Angeles, and Washington, DC all simultaneously. Especially if you are recruiting non-Arabs now. You have a factory here, to make explosives?"

He didn't answer, but his face said they had. I leaned across the table toward him.

"Tell me if I am scaring you, Gabbai, but this is how we operate in the Regiment. We don't sit around conversing with God and scratching our asses. We get things done. How many guys have you got here right now?" I didn't let him answer. "I'll tell you why I'm asking. You tell me, if Andrei and one of his pals was to take a hundred pounds of C4 down to DC and blow the front out of every Bank of America Financial Center in DC, on the very day I kill the brigadier, two generals, and a rear admiral. How would that be? Take a little time to prepare, and you could fly a drone loaded with C4 into the Capitol Building, or any number of other targets." He was frowning hard at me, and you could see he was interested in what I was saying. I said, "Come on, how many guys you got here right now?"

"Six."

"So get your brother to bring six more guys to keep a watch on me and Chelsea, and let me do my job. You will have the biggest score of your career!"

"Strike at the Capitol...?"

I made a face. "That needs proper preparation. You know what? I'd target the federal reserve. Park a car outside with a hundred pounds of C4 in it. You don't even need to kill anyone. You hit the banks, the big financial institutions, and you can write your own ticket."

He raised both hands and gave a small laugh. "Your enthusiasm is commendable, Harry, but let us get this first job done, and then we will plan others."

I stood. "Suit yourself, but you hit the Bank of America in DC at the same time and you multiply your impact several hundred percent. Let me show you something—"

I stepped around the table as I spoke. He was frowning and went to stand as I approached. I waved my left hand at him. "No, don't get up. Look, look at this—"

It was a single, fluid movement I had practiced a thousand times. It was muscle memory. I wrapped my left arm around his head and clamped my left hand over his mouth while I drew the Fairbairn-Sykes from my boot. They'd gotten my hunting knife and my Sig, but they never thought about my fighting knife.

I rammed the razor sharp point into his neck, driving through his carotid artery, and when it was fully home up to the hilt, I punched hard forward, severing his esophagus and his windpipe. There was a grotesque eruption of blood from his throat across the table, but by the time Sergei had looked around, gaped for three seconds and gotten to his feet, I had Gabbai's Glock 17 in my hand and put three rounds into his chest.

Five left. One of them was outside, watching the entrance to the cave. I'd already had an encounter with him when I arrived. I peered out the window and saw no activity. So I figured he'd keep.

That left four, and the tramping of boots told me that, unlike their pal outside, they'd heard the shots. I had no time to think or prepare, so I dropped on the floor behind Gabbai's boots and aimed at the doorway through which they would have to enter.

But the acoustics of the cave had thrown me a curve ball, and the four troopers burst in through the front door of the cabin. One of them stood gaping at Sergei lying sprawled on the floor. Two stood gaping at the horrible mess on the dining table. The fourth stood staring at me on the floor.

He pointed at me and screamed something in Russian. I shot him through the head, and the guy next to him winced, covering his head with his arm as his pal's brains splattered his face. I fired again, but by then they were storming at me, screaming, shooting, and kicking.

SIXTEEN

I SAY SHOOTING, BUT REALLY IT WAS JUST ONE shot, because after that, they all got in each other's way. But they were screaming and kicking. I got kicked in the ribs and in the belly. Then my leg was stamped on, and my arm, trying to make me let go of the Glock. It was a matter of seconds, then one of them had me lined up, and everything slowed down. All I could see was their frenzied faces as they were stamping and kicking, the guy holding his pistol in both hands with wild eyes and spit on his lips, and the certainty in my chest that I was less than a second from death.

Time warped or something. I fired the Glock and hit his weapon. The ricochet tore through the face of the guy next to him. They both screamed, and I tried to scramble to my feet. I got a savage kick in my hip and went down again with long silver needles of pain piercing my back. As I hit the floor, he came in for another kick, and I knew that one would finish me. The guy with the ripped face was just behind him, screaming blue murder.

I didn't aim. I just fired six shots like crazy in their direction. One round went right through what was left of Torn Face's face and exploded out the back of his head. Four went astray, but the sixth hit the guy who was kicking me. It hit him right in the knee, and he went down screaming like a parrot with a hornet up its ass. I got to my feet. The guy who was going to shoot me was trying to grip his weapon, but his hands had swollen to twice their size. I pulled the fighting knife from my boot, stepped over to him, and shoved it through his throat, splitting his spinal cord in the back of his neck.

Then I turned to the guy with the shattered knee.

"You speak English?"

He stared at me, sobbing. I knelt beside him. "You want to live?"

He nodded.

"Are there any more men?"

"No. Only us. All dead now."

"You are not dead. Help me and you can live. Is there a room or a cave where you make explosives?"

He nodded. "Yes."

"Where?"

"Go out, behind, there is cave open and inside big laboratory."

"Anybody there?"

"I tell you, yes? I collaborating with you. You no kill me."

"No, I no kill you. Who is there?"

"Two tech-nee, tech-nee-thians."

"That's it?"

"Yes, no more."

I cut the carotid artery in his neck, and his death was quick and relatively painless.

I collected a couple of weapons as backup and headed out the cabin door. I followed his direction, skirting the rubble and boulders where the cabin had been built, and found a long, vertical opening in the rocks through which amber light filtered. I walked in and found two men in their late forties. They both wore white lab coats. One had a paunch and a double chin which he concealed behind an abundant, scraggly beard. He had heavy glasses with thick lenses that made his eyes look very small and round.

His pal was taller and skinny with a bald head and a mustache. They both stared at me. I was going to ask them if they spoke English and what they made there, but I could see what it was. It was plastic explosive, and you didn't need to be Sherlock Holmes to work out it was being stockpiled.

I didn't feel too bad about shooting two unarmed technicians. I figured if they were prepared to stockpile enough high grade plastic explosives to take out a city block and all the people in and around it, then they were probably the kind of trash I was born to take out.

I shot them both in the head and spent the next hour transporting, stacking, and positioning about a hundred pounds of the stuff in and around the cabin. I am no explosives expert, but I was pretty confident the way I had laid it out would bring down enough of the ceiling of the cave to block the place for good. I found a box of remote detonators in the lab and went to find Chelsea.

She was still asleep. I woke her gently, and when she opened her eyes and focused on me, I said, "We're leaving."

She frowned. "Already? I don't understand."

"It doesn't matter. Just get dressed. We're going."

She slipped out of bed and padded toward the bathroom on bare feet.

I said, "Don't bother showering. Just get dressed. We're leaving now."

She turned and frowned at me. "What's going on?"

"I'm not going to tell you a third time. Get dressed. Now."

She blinked. Her expression shifted from confused and sleepy to worried. She pulled on her clothes in silence. When she had laced her boots, she said, "Are you going to tell me what's going on?"

"No. And as we go through the cabin, I want you to keep your eyes closed."

"What the hell...?"

"Just do it, Chelsea. Stop arguing."

Lot might have said the same to his wife and gotten the same result. I'd have done better putting a pillowcase over her head. As soon as we got to the cabin, she opened her eyes and looked around. I watched her face and saw all the blood drain from it. Her voice came out as barely a whisper.

"My God, Harry, what have you done?"

I grabbed her and shoved her toward the door. "We haven't got time for this. Move!"

I dragged her at a stumbling run across the long cavern. The light at the opening was a dull grainy blue, and I knew night was falling. We made it out of the cave and scrambled down the steep, sandy slope, following the rough path I had noticed from above, when I had first arrived. I kept Chelsea just ahead of me as we went.

When we reached the shore, in the dying light it was hard to tell where the path went. But I was pretty sure from when I had seen it earlier that it turned left, toward Freemont Lake. I pointed. "That way."

She picked her way along the shoreline, among the dense undergrowth that fed on the cold water of the lake. Soon, as I had expected, we came across a large rowing boat with two sets of oars and room for at least six people.

She watched me drag it out onto the water. I said, "Get in," and she did as I said almost like an automaton. As I pushed the boat over the last couple of feet of gravel and into the dark water and jumped in to take the oars, she bent forward and buried her face in her hands and started to sob violently. I left her to it, pulled the detonator from my pocket, and pressed the red button. There was a muted thud in the air. Then a roar and flame as smoke and rocks exploded from the mouth of the cave to rain down on the lake like a smoldering shower of meteorites.

Chelsea looked up with wide eyes and stared at the smoking mouth of the cave. Then her gaze dropped to the surface of the water, where the last, steaming rocks were falling. Then she turned to stare at me.

I ignored her and rowed steadily toward the western shore of Long Lake, where Freemont Creek spills in from the mountains above. It was a good mile. I was more interested in being quiet than fast, so it was maybe eight minutes before the bow of the boat crunched on the loose gravel and I was able to jump ashore and drag her in among the pines.

I took Chelsea's hand and helped her out. When she was standing in front of me, I held her shoulders and looked hard into her eyes. In the growing dark, beside the icy waters of the lake and the creek, it was growing real cold, and she was beginning to shudder.

"I need you to listen to me. Nobody is going to follow us." I saw her eyes half close. "We are no longer in danger from people. But out here, there are bears and wolves, so I need you to stay alert for me until we get to the trailhead. Do you understand me?"

She nodded. I took off my jacket and put it around her shoulders.

"We are just one and a half miles from the Jeep. If we stay focused and keep up a good pace, we can make it in less than two hours. Can you do that?"

She nodded, pulling the jacket close around her, and we set off, following a deep gulley that led from the Long Lake up an ever steeper, wooded incline toward the trailhead. A mile or a mile and a half in town or even in farmed country-side is not a big deal, and you could probably walk it in half an hour. But at night, in the foothills of the Wind River Mountains, with no trail to follow, stumbling over fallen trees, loose rocks and shrubs, it's the equivalent of a ten-mile hike. And though I'd told her less than two hours, I knew it was more likely to be three, and the farther we went, the more exhausted she would become, with cold and shock sapping her energy.

I didn't know what time we had left the cave. The sun had already set and dusk was turning to evening, so I figured it must have been eight or eight-thirty. By the time we finally found a track, followed it to the Sacred Rim trailhead, and found the Jeep still parked there, it was well after eleven-thirty. Chelsea climbed in the passenger seat, hunched forward, and began to sob violently. I didn't waste time. I got behind the wheel and began the steady drive home. The temptation to hit the gas was strong, and when I could see there was no traffic and we were alone, I did, but the risk of getting stopped by some deputy was too great, and it was another half hour before I was able to park outside my house, take Chelsea inside, wrap her in blankets on the sofa, and give her a mug of hot chocolate, generously laced with whiskey.

There she sobbed herself to sleep.

When she was snoring softly, I called the brigadier.

"Harry. Any news?"

"Yeah. This setup is more complex than we thought. Intiquaam is what Gabbai called their battle cry."

"You met him and spoke to him?"

"Yeah. He recruited me. The organization is called aldam bialdam."

"Blood for blood."

"Yeah, they've had an HQ in a cave in the Wind River Mountains since nine-eleven with an explosives factory. He told me they had been liaising with billionaires in Jackson Hole during this time. But by the quantity of plastic explosives I found there, I'd say they were building up to something."

"Where are you now?"

"I'm back home. The whole crew are dead except Chelsea. They killed them all. I killed all of them, including Gabbai, and I used their explosives to seal the cave."

"Good man. But—"

"We need to meet, sir. At my place in New York."

"Can you tell me anything more?"

"No. Not now. But we need to meet with General John Moorcroft, General Schwarz, and Admiral Sam Benner."

"I see."

"I have arranged with Del, Mohammed Ben-Amini's nephew, Gabbai's brother, to meet in New York in the next few days. We should meet before that."

"All right, Harry. You get some rest tonight. Let me know your ETA tomorrow, and I'll arrange it with John and Sam and company."

"Good, thank you, sir. I'll talk to you tomorrow."

I hung up and sat a while looking at my phone. After a moment I said quietly, to myself, "Good bye, sir. End of an era. Blood for bloody blood."

I slipped the cell in my pocket and went out on the deck and sat on the steps. It was a matter of maybe fifteen seconds before I saw the Kiwi emerge from the shadows by the garage and walk toward me. He spoke like quiet gravel.

"You always did like blowing things up."

"It's my repressed Oedipal complex."

He sat next to me and fished a crumpled pack of Camel from his shirt pocket. "You have to be careful with the Oedipal complex. It can make you blind."

I smiled. "Droll."

"When I saw you go in, I guessed you knew what you were doing, in as much as you ever do, and went and escorted Allivya and company to the trailhead."

"I figured."

"By the time I got back, you were making your getaway. What's the state of play?"

"Gabbai's dead. He and all his pals are enjoying a total of six hundred and thirty virgins."

He shook his head and sighed. "I never did get the thing with virgins. In my humble opinion, there is something to be said for experience. What about your lady?"

I jabbed a thumb over my shoulder. "In shock, asleep on the sofa. We fly to New York tomorrow. Del is going to pay me ten million dollars and a beach house in Belize to give him Buddy's head, along with the heads of General John Moorcroft, General Schwarz, and Admiral Sam Benner."

"Son of a bitch."

He'd been fiddling with the cigarette while we spoke. Now he put it in his mouth and lit it with a silver Zippo that sported a skull and crossbones. He took a deep drag, and I told him, "All my life, Kiwi, I've been doing what other people tell me, obeying orders, killing to suit other people's ambitions and objectives. Now it's my turn. You know? I want my ten million bucks, I want a beautiful, five bedroom house on the beach, with a swimming pool, and I want my woman to share it with."

He nodded and looked at the tip of his cigarette. "I hear you, bro."

"Either one of us kills the other right now or you join me. We go fifty-fifty. Hell, you come along and we can screw another fifty mil out of him. What do you say? Are you in?"

"You aim to kill Buddy and the generals?"

"I don't want to. Buddy was the best officer I ever knew, and he was a friend. But we both know Buddy. He won't let this go. Besides, Del wants their heads. We have to show him the heads before he pays."

"Agreed. And when we hand over the heads, we persuade them to pay us a bonus."

"That's the plan."

He spat into his right hand, and we shook.

"I'm in," he said.

SEVENTEEN

WE TOOK AN AIR TAXI FROM THE RALPH WENZ airport south of Pinedale to New Jersey and arrived at my brownstone in the early afternoon. Chelsea had hardly spoken since the day before, and when we arrived at my place, she showered and went straight to bed in one of the guest rooms without lunch and without saying anything to me.

I spent the afternoon in the gym in the basement, and at five-thirty, my phone rang. It was an unknown number.

"Yeah?"

"Mr. Bauer? Harry Bauer?"

"Yes."

"This is Del. My brother called me yesterday regarding your requirements."

"I was there when he called you. You agreed. Are you in New York?"

"Yes, I am in New York. We should get together for a preliminary meeting this evening. What do you say?"

"Where?"

"You will come to my apartment on Central Park West, three twenty-two. The entrance is on West 92nd, but the address is Central Park. I have the penthouse. There we will discuss the details and precisely how we proceed."

"Where and at what time?"

"Park Lane"—he gave me the address—"at seven p.m. Bring your woman. We can have dinner."

"We are not becoming bosom pals, Del. This is business, and that's where it stays."

"And can't we talk business over dinner? Bring your woman. We will have dinner and discuss the future."

"Let's be clear about this, Del. I am burning my bridges and betraying the best, most efficient killers on the planet, and I will be killing one of their best loved officers. The change of identity, ten million bucks, and the house in Belize are not negotiable. And I want five million up front before I swat a damned fly."

"That is perfectly understood. We will see you at seven this evening."

I hung up, poured myself a whiskey, and called the brigadier.

"Harry, where are you?"

"I'm back home in New York. Can I expect you tomorrow evening, with General Moorcroft, General Schwarz, and Admiral Sam Benner?"

"Yes, though I do wish you could give me a clearer idea of what it's about."

"Yeah, me too. But I don't want to discuss it over the phone."

"Shall I come over now?"

"No. I have a meeting at seven with Del. I'll probably be there all evening. I'll explain everything tomorrow evening."

"Are you all right, Harry?"

"Sure. I'll see you tomorrow."

I climbed the stairs to Chelsea's room and walked in without knocking. I stood over her, and after a moment she frowned and blinked and opened her eyes. After a moment, she sat up and said, "What is it?"

"I'm going out. I'll be back around midnight."

"Where are you going?"

"I'm going to meet Del to make arrangements."

Her cheeks colored, and she bit her lip. "You're going through with this, then?"

"I have to."

She shook her head. "Harry, I don't want you to do this. He's your friend. I've heard how you talk to him. Can't we just go somewhere—"

"No. They'd find us. This is the only way."

"Then I want to come with you."

"What for?"

Her face screwed up in frustration. "Why are you being like this? You're treating me as though all of this is my fault!"

I sighed, walked to the chair by the window, and sat with my elbows on my knees. After a long moment, I spoke.

"I have lost everyone who has mattered to me. They have either been killed because of my job, or they have left because of my job. I don't want you to get hurt. I don't want..." I trailed off, clasped my hands, and looked down at the floor. "Nothing can ever happen between us. If it did, you wouldn't stay. And if you stayed, you would probably get killed. All I can do is protect you as best I can and stop you from getting involved. You cannot be involved in my life."

She was shaking her head. "What about this ten million dollars, and the house in Belize? That was for us."

"It was and is for you. I can't be any part of your life. When I take possession of the house, I'll sell it, and the proceeds will be for you. So you can make a new start."

She was quiet for a long while, staring at me, frowning. "I don't understand, Harry. You would do all this for me? You hardly know me. I mean," she faltered. "We were attracted to each other, and we slept together, but this... You would really do this for me? Why?"

I shook my head. "Don't ask stupid questions I can't answer." I stood and sighed. "I will do this for you because a four-year-old child was raped and murdered in Afghanistan, and there was nothing I could do to help her. Maybe, in a normal, sane world, I would allow myself to have feelings for you and I would do this because of those feelings. But this is not a normal, sane world. This is a world which is sick and infirm and twisted. So the best I can do for you is stay away from you."

She got out of bed and came and knelt in front of me, took a hold of my hands, and looked up into my face.

"That's wrong, Harry. I—" She faltered. "I have never been in a situation like this. I have never known anyone like you. I don't know what's going on—around me *or* inside me. But I do know that I am not going to just walk away and dump you. I am coming with you tonight. And I will stand by you through this."

I closed my eyes and sighed deeply. "I told you not to

encourage those kids to come along. You didn't listen to me and look what happened."

"Harry, that is not fair! That was a stupid mistake, and I learned my lesson."

"I am warning you now that getting close to me is dangerous. I am warning you not to do it."

"This is different. It is my personal choice, and it affects only me. I am coming with you, and I am going to stand by your side!"

"OK." I sighed again with a heavy feeling deep in my chest. "You'd better get dressed."

I stood, and she stood with me, moved forward, and pressed against me. "Get dressed?" she breathed in my ear. "Right now?"

———

I FOUND a space to park not too far from the back, and we took the elevator up to the penthouse which occupied the whole top floor. The elevator stopped in the entrance hall of the apartment.

When the doors hissed open, there was a large guy in a white jacket and white gloves waiting to receive us. His eyes slid over Chelsea, then he turned to me.

"You are Mr. Harry Bauer?"

"Yeah."

"Please follow me."

He led us through highly polished double doors that looked like solid walnut and down a short passage which was wide enough to drive a Dodge RAM through. At the end, another set of identical doors opened onto a large space that included a dining area and a drawing room. The far wall was all plate glass with views across a terracotta terrace to the Jackie Kennedy Reservoir.

The rest of the place was ninety percent empty space, and the ten percent that was furnished looked like the spawn from a nightmare shared by Salvador Dali and the Marquis de Sade. Not that they depicted scenes of sadistic torture in melting landscapes, but the six chairs at the glass table, each shaped like a unique frozen flame, seemed designed for the specific purpose of making you uncomfortable for the duration of your meal. The transparent table itself looked more like a razorblade than a place where you would want to eat.

The drawing room, which was beside the vast glass wall, was a cold, desolate landscape with chairs that looked like plants from an early episode of Star Trek. There was a sofa that had no back and no arms, and there were no lamp tables or coffee table to put your glass. It was the kind of place you immediately wanted to leave.

The guy in the white coat stood at the open doors and said in a big voice, "Mr. Harry Bauer and his woman," then turned and left. There was a movement in the sparse drawing room area, and a man emerged from one of the chairs. He held a newspaper in his hand and dropped it on the floor as he moved toward us. He must have been thirty feet away, but he didn't hurry. He was smiling and spoke as he walked.

"Harry Bauer," he said. "A mere sergeant you were, but what a warrior. So much pain you caused us. I have wanted so long to kill you and avenge our fallen brothers." He stopped just three feet from me and clasped my shoulders. "But now you are redeemed, called to the bosom of Allah."

He laughed suddenly and very loudly, slapping me on the shoulders as he did so. "And what better vengeance for me, eh, Harry? What better vengeance than to make you my servant?"

He laughed again, and I thought how easy it would be to kill him right then and be done. I could break his neck and walk out. It was tempting, but I knew it was not enough. If this was going to be finished, it had to be finished right. I thought about his brother in the cave in the Winds, and that made me smile.

"You done?"

He gestured toward the weird, ugly seats. "Come, have a drink."

"Do we have to drink mint tea or can we have a real drink?"

He chuckled as he settled himself in a wicker thing that looked like a carnivorous plant. "Oh, I think Allah will forgive us if we make a small exception in honor of our new convert."

Chelsea sat in a red plastic bowl, and I straddled something that looked like a Swedish IKEA recliner.

"My woman will have a vodka martini. I'll have a Bushmills straight up. I want extraction for me and my woman tomorrow to Mexico, and I want you to come along with us to keep us company."

"That is not a problem, my friend." He pressed a button on the arm of his chair and spoke in Arabic. Then he looked at me with large brown eyes. "Tell me what is your plan so that I can arrange your extraction."

"My plan is simple. Brigadier Alexander Byrd, Army General John Moorcroft, of the Joint Chiefs of Staff,

General Schwarz of the Marines, a personal advisor to the president, and Admiral Sam Benner, also advisor to the president, are all coming to dinner tomorrow evening at my house. They believe I am going to brief them on you and your organization, aldam bialdam. Instead I am going to kill them all. I will remove their heads and put them in a large box, which I shall deliver to you upon extraction. When I am ready, I will send you a signal. You pick me up at my front door."

I glanced at Chelsea. She looked unhappy.

"Chelsea stays with you. When you pick me up at my house, I want to see her in the car. If she has been hurt or treated disrespectfully, I will kill you, the driver, and anybody else who happens to be in the car. You will pay me five million dollars tonight on account, and tomorrow, when you see the heads, you will pay me the other five million."

He thought about it. "You want me to pick you up at your front door. How do I know I will not be stormed by police or special operatives outside your house?"

"As soon as the job is done, I'll send you a photograph. When I step out of that door, I will have a carton containing four heads. I am going to make damn sure there are no cops and no special operatives around. You just make damn sure you have your laptop with you so you can make the transfer."

The drinks were served, and we spent half an hour discussing details, mainly aimed at ensuring that I did not cheat them and they did not cheat me. When our drinks were finished, Del rose and gestured toward the dining area. We followed him, and I saw that the table had been set. There was a silver ice bucket containing a bottle of champagne, and beside his place at the head of the table, there was an open laptop built into an attaché case standing open. Del gestured to it.

"You see, my friend, it is all ready. Five million dollars. You just introduce your account, I will review it, and you have your five million on account, and tomorrow, when I see their heads, you will get the other half." I approached the computer and examined the screen. It appeared to be what he said it was. The bank was in Panama, which was no great surprise. I entered my account, which appeared as a series of asterisks, and gestured to Del to authorize the transactions. He did so, and after a moment, he said, "Please, Harry, check your account and tell me if the money has been credited."

I checked my bank on my cell, and after a couple of seconds, the transfer was confirmed. I nodded to him. He poured champagne, and we toasted. I sipped and told him, "I always find it easier to trust a man after he has paid me five million bucks."

He laughed. "Who can argue with that? Please, sit, let us dine."

We dined on smoked salmon, lamb, couscous, dates, and goat cheese. The food was good and the chairs were not as uncomfortable as they looked, and after a couple of glasses of wine, we had relaxed enough to hold a normal conversation and pretend we were enjoying ourselves.

Throughout the evening, he did not address a word to Chelsea, and at eleven o'clock, when I rose to leave, she stood and with frightened eyes, moved toward me.

"You're not going to leave me here, are you?"

I held her by the shoulders and looked into her eyes. "I'm sorry. You are their insurance against my going rogue.

They know that as long as they have you, I'll play the game." I shifted my gaze to Del. "But they also know that if they hurt you, there will be blood to pay. Aldam bialdam."

He smiled on one side of his face. "You have nothing to fear, Harry. You are one of us now. We will treat your property with all the respect which we owe to you. Which is considerable. You may go in peace."

I turned back to Chelsea. "I'll see you tomorrow evening. And then we start a whole new life."

She nodded but gripped me as I turned to go. "Harry, I'm scared."

Del spoke to me. "She will have a beautiful room with handmaids to care for her. She will sleep well, and she will not be disturbed. Tomorrow we will take her to meet you when you notify us."

I gave her a kiss. "I'll see you tomorrow."

EIGHTEEN

The brigadier arrived at seven p.m. accompanied by Admiral Sam Benner, General Schwarz, and Army General John Moorcroft, of the Joint Chiefs of Staff. Their attempt to be inconspicuous involved not wearing uniforms but arriving together in a Cadillac limousine. The car that was parked across the road with two young Arab males reading newspapers was about as inconspicuous as the Pentagon's finest and their Caddy.

I showed them into the living room, seated them, and poured drinks. I handed the brigadier his Bushmills, and they all watched me sit like they were waiting for something. The brigadier waited a moment, then raised his glass.

"Cheers." After he'd sipped, he said, "Have you got something to tell us?"

I nodded a few times, not looking at him but at the floor.

"Gabbai is dead. The field headquarters they'd had at Sacred Rim in the Wind River Mountains for the last twenty-four years is destroyed. Out of the dozen or so men I killed, maybe a third were Arabs. The rest seemed to be Russian. They had a lab there in which they were manufacturing industrial amounts of plastic explosives, but Gabbai told me their main function—their main purpose for being in that part of Wyoming was to be close enough to Jackson Hole to make contact with the large number of billionaires who inhabit that area and occupy very large, remote ranches. He didn't give me any names."

General Moorcroft muttered, "Jesus Christ!"

"It gets better. Del is still alive. He is not aware yet that his brother is dead, or the Wind River field headquarters has been destroyed. He heads up an organization called aldam bialdam—"

The brigadier nodded. "Blood for blood."

"Right. Their battle cry is Intiquaam, revenge, but their brief goes well beyond what we thought. We thought they were out to punish our patrol in the Helmand Province. But their purpose is much greater than that. They are out to seek revenge against the West, and especially the United States and the United Kingdom for what they see as our aggression in the Middle East after nine-eleven and for our support of Israel against the Palestinians. They want blood for blood on a massive scale." I shook my head. "When I took out the cave in the Winds, I just took out the regional office. The head office is still fully functional in Afghanistan, Iran, or maybe even Russia."

General Schwarz interrupted me.

"But the Afghans—the Taliban—are Sunni, but Iran is Shiite. I can't see a Sunni organization having its main headquarters in a Shiite state like Iran."

I nodded. "Up until this week, I would have agreed. But like

I said earlier, two-thirds of the guys I came up against were not even Arabs. Del is modeling his organization on the Hashishim. He is somehow transcending national and religious barriers and focusing on Allah, Mohammed, and the jihad. This is a very dangerous, insidious organization, and if what Gabbai told me is true, they already have tendrils deep inside Congress, the Senate, and the financial powerbase of the United States."

Admiral Benner was frowning hard at me. "This is a lot of very detailed intelligence, Harry. How did you learn so much in such a short time?"

I turned to him and took a deep breath. I took a sip of my whiskey, and after a moment I told him, "Because they recruited me."

The admiral arched an eyebrow. "You want to run that by me again?"

"Before I killed him, Gabbai recruited me into aldam bialdam as an assassin."

They all glanced at each other, but the brigadier kept watching me, frowning. "Harry, what reason would they have for believing you would be loyal? What reason would they have for trusting you?"

"More than one," I told him. "They offered me ten million dollars, a change of identity, and a big, beautiful house on the beach in Belize. They are also holding Chelsea hostage, and if I don't do what they have instructed me to do, they will torture her, rape her, and kill her."

The silence was a palpable thing in the room. Eventually it was the brigadier who asked the sixty-four thousand dollar question: "What have they instructed you to do?"

"Kill you, behead you, and deliver your heads to Del."

"They are holding Chelsea hostage? The television producer? What are you going to do?"

I shrugged with my eyebrows, stood, and made my way to the drinks tray. There I set down my glass and turned to face them.

"I just told you," I said, and pulled the Sig from under my arm.

They stared at me, unbelieving and uncomprehending. I shot the brigadier first, in the center of his forehead. Army General John Moorcroft, of the Joint Chiefs of Staff, was next. Then General Schwarz of the Marines, personal advisor to the president, and finally Admiral Sam Benner, also advisor to the president. It was in rapid succession, one, two three, four. It took maybe two or three seconds, and it was all over. They sat there in their chairs, slumped, astonished, dead.

I put away the Sig, pulled my cell from my pocket, and took a photograph of each one of them. I sent the photographs to Del and went to the kitchen for the knife I had sharpened and the large box I had prepared.

Fifteen minutes later, I closed the blood-smeared carton and tied it with string. Then I climbed the stairs to the bathroom, taking care to touch nothing on the way. Then I stood under the shower for twenty minutes, scrubbing my hands and body with soap long after the last traces of blood were gone from my hands.

Downstairs I collected the slugs and the shells and slipped them in a polythene bag, which I fixed to the bag with adhesive tape.

Finally I made two calls. The first was to an acquaintance

in New York. He answered the phone without speaking. That was his style.

I said, "I had a party and I need a cleaning service."

"How many?"

"Three."

"Give me half an hour."

"Listen, this is a private matter, OK? If this gets out, I'll know where the leak is and I'll plug it. You understand me."

"Yeah, fuck you. I know my job."

"Send me the bill. Add some for discretion."

He hung up without answering. I called Del.

"Yeah."

"I'm ready."

I picked up the box. It was surprisingly heavy. I stepped out onto the stoop and let the door thud closed behind me. There was something final about the click of the latch, and I knew, suddenly, with certainty, that I was close to death. If it came—when it came—I wondered what it would be like. A transition into something else? Or a simple switching off of the lights?

Two dark SUVs with smoked windows turned into the street, moved silently along, and came to a halt at the bottom of the stairs. The side door of the front one slid open, and I carried the box down. I slung it in and climbed in after it to sit opposite Del and next to a six-four gorilla in a suit. Chelsea was sitting next to Del, looking like she felt sick.

"You couldn't find a less discrete vehicle? Something with strip lighting on the roof that said, 'We just killed two generals, a brigadier, and an admiral'?"

He smiled. "Relax. This is America. Everybody looks like a dangerous killer. It is the national hobby."

We turned south on Fifth Avenue, and Del gestured with both hands at the box. "This is it?"

"You wanted me to wrap it with a pink bow? What's the matter with you? Of course that's it. Open it and have a look. Now I want five million bucks and a flight out of Teterboro Airport."

"Harry, Harry. You seem stressed. It is normal after killing an old friend and betraying your country." He smiled like he really hoped he was hurting me. "Even if that betrayal is for God. But relax. You are one of us now, and we will look after you. We are more powerful than you might think."

I nodded. "Good. I'm glad to hear that."

He had the attaché case by his feet. He pulled it onto his lap, opened it, and pulled out a large manila envelope, which he handed to me. I opened it and pulled out a sheaf of photographs of a cute, five-bedroom house on a white, sandy beach. The rear of the house was enclosed by trees, including palms and banana trees. Along with the photographs was the certificate of registration for the property in my name. There were also two sets of keys and two tickets, one for me and one for Chelsea.

I looked at Del. "What about you? I told Gabbai I wanted you—"

He reached in his inside pocket and pulled out a ticket. "Relax. Everything is as you wanted it."

I pointed at the laptop. "Not yet." He drew breath, but I shook my head. "When we get to Teterboro. We have some things to discuss."

Del scowled at me. "What things? Don't start playing games, Harry. The consequences will be ugly."

"Who's getting their knickers in a twist now, Del? Take

it easy. I have some questions about the future, nothing more than that. But I want to discuss it over a cup of coffee. That's all."

He didn't answer. We moved in silence through the late evening traffic, across the massive, dark river and onto I-95. Five minutes later, we pulled into the small airport and parked outside the private lounge. Dell took a moment to look at me.

"The jet is waiting to take us to Belize."

I nodded once. "This won't take long. Bring the gorilla but tell your other boys to wait outside."

He sat forward with his elbows on his knees. His eyes were dead.

"I am running out of patience, Harry. If you think my men will not kill you in a public place, you are very mistaken."

"Thanks for letting me know, Del. Nobody is going to get killed this evening. We just need to clarify some details. Your boys will be right outside. You OK or are you scared? You want Mommy to come and hold your hand?"

He grunted and climbed out of the SUV. He spoke some words in Arabic to the driver of the other SUV and followed me toward the lounge.

Inside I saw the Kiwi sitting in an armchair at a coffee table reading the *Economist*. He dropped the magazine on the table as I approached and looked up at Del and his ape-man. He ignored Chelsea.

Del was beginning to look real mad. Ape-man had brain constipation. His brows were knotted, and he looked like if he really strained, a thought might come out. Del said, "Who is this?"

"This is the Kiwi. He's the other member of our patrol you didn't manage to kill. We work together. Sit down or I'll kill your gorilla and the Kiwi will rip your throat out. All we want is to make a deal. You benefit and we benefit. Sit down, Del."

He took a moment but sat. "What deal?"

Chelsea sat too, but the gorilla remained standing. It was the Kiwi who answered Del.

"The brigadier was like our godfather. He looked after us, took care of us and, what is most important in this particular case, Del, we could trust him. Now he's gone. What can I say, life sucks and in our profession you learn to be ruthless when you have to be, right? You score a big publicity bonanza in the media and the social media, you get a huge recruiting drive. This is your biggest hit since nine-eleven. In many ways it's bigger, because it is a direct hit at the heart of the enemy, using the enemy's own men. But"—he shrugged and spread his hands—"what do we get? One house and ten million bucks shared three ways."

Del's eyes flashed to me. I smiled. He said, "What do you want?"

I said, "So this comes in two parts. First of all, we need ten million bucks each, plus two million each for these two so they can buy themselves decent living accommodation. So we are looking at a total payoff of twenty-nine million backs right here and now. We are aware you might refuse to pay. But you should remember, Del, that we are desperate men with nothing to lose, and we are very, very good at killing. So if you call your men, you and your gorilla will be dead before they get to the door. You are holding the box with the heads, and we will be the heroes who stopped you before you left the country. Make the transfer, and we will be available for future jobs—Congress? The Pentagon? The White House...?"

It took him ten long seconds. But he took the attaché case, opened it, did some typing, and handed it to me. I checked the screen. It was no different than the one before. The Kiwi had gotten to his feet and had his eye on the door. I tapped in the account number and hit send. After a couple of seconds, my cell pinged and told me I had received the transfer.

I stood.

"OK, you enjoy your flight. We will be making our own way, and we will take care of our own ID changes." I held up the manila envelope. "You know where you can contact me. I will see you there in a couple of days, and we can discuss the next job." I smiled at him. "Be good, and if not, be careful."

I grabbed Chelsea by the arm and pulled her to her feet. We exited the lounge into the parking lot and made for a Land Rover at the far end. I smiled and saluted the guys in the SUV. My gut told me Del was still trying to make sense of the turn of events and hadn't decided yet whether to have us killed or not. The Kiwi got behind the wheel and fired up the engine, I bundled Chelsea into the front passenger seat, and I got in the back with my Sig in my hand.

We waited almost five minutes. The Kiwi said, "They're getting in the SUV."

I watched the lights come on and the vehicle pulled out of the lot and onto Industrial Avenue. A minute after that, I watched Del leave the lounge and cross the tarmac toward his waiting jet.

"He accepted the invitation to the next job," I said. "He's boarding the jet."

We waited another five minutes while it turned and taxied to the runway. The engines began to howl, and after a moment, the small Gulfstream began its sprint along the black strip. I already had my cell in my hand. I pressed nine on the keypad, and the jet erupted in a massive fireball, hurling bits of twisted, burning steel spiraling into the air, while inside, Del, his gorilla, and the aircrew were incinerated where they sat.

The Kiwi sighed as he spun the wheel and headed for the exit.

"I always said, you know, under that cold, English exterior, the brigadier was a bit hot-headed."

NINETEEN

WE DROVE IN SILENCE THROUGH THE NIGHT, UP I-95 and across the bridge back into Manhattan. Chelsea sat motionless, staring ahead at the road as it unfolded.

When we'd crossed the George Washington, we took Amsterdam as far as Martin Luther King and turned east. I noticed then that Chelsea was beginning to frown and look around. When we crossed Fifth and turned north onto Madison, she said, "Where are we going? This is..."

She trailed off. I said, "We're going to my place. I've had the cleaners in."

She turned to look at me. Her face expressed disgust. "How can you?"

"What's the alternative? We go to a motel? And when the Feds and the Secret Service come knocking, I explain I had the four of them here, they disappeared, and I went out to a motel? You're going to do this kind of shit you keep a cold head and make it work."

Her eyes narrowed. "My God, what kind of monster are you?"

"The kind who's had enough of being used and exploited for other people's gain and benefit. The kind that has decided, if I keep killing, it's for my benefit. Not anybody else's. And before you go condemning me, you might take a moment to consider that if you are alive right now, it's thanks to me."

She didn't answer. We made a left onto 129th and then another left onto 5th Avenue. A third took us onto 128th, and the Kiwi pulled up outside my brownstone. I swung down and opened the front passenger door. Chelsea stared down at me, and there was real fear in her eyes.

"Are you going to kill me?"

"If that was in my mind, don't you think I would have done it by now? No, the Kiwi has stuff he has to do. Tomorrow the three of us are flying to Belize. I need to transfer his share of the money to him and yours to you, and there's stuff I need to explain to you. Come on, you must have seen by now that I am not going to hurt you."

The Kiwi leaned over and growled in her ear, "If we'd wanted to hurt you, we would not have brought you here. We'd have taken you to Soundview Park and dumped you in the East River."

She turned to stare at him, then climbed down from the truck. I slammed the door, raised my hand to the Kiwi, and he drove away. Chelsea followed me to the stoop and climbed the stairs.

In the living room, she stood staring at the chairs and the carpet. I watched her a moment, then said, "I told you, I had the cleaners in."

She turned suddenly and stared at me, frowning. I explained.

"When you kill people for a living, you end up using cleaning services. They are professionals. Some of them are forensic experts. They come in after the kill, and they clean up. I took the shells and the slugs, and I gave them to Del as proof I'd done the job."

"Where are the—" She stopped like she couldn't say the word.

"The bodies?" She nodded. "The cleaners took them in the van. You need a drink? I could use one."

She didn't answer. So I walked to the bookcase where there was a tray of decanters and glasses and poured her a strong martini and myself a stiff Bushmills. I handed it to her, and she stared at it a moment, like she didn't know what it was. Then she frowned and took it.

"I don't understand," she said at last. "What did you do? You put a bomb in with their *heads*?"

I shrugged. "It makes habeas corpus a bit tricky, right? And also gets rid of a man who would certainly have gone all out to punish me when he discovered I d killed his brother and destroyed his outfit in the Winds. And you know as well as I do what punish means. Death would be a final release."

"You killed them. One of them was your friend. You cut off their heads and put them in a box, and then placed a bomb in with the heads."

"Yes."

She crossed the room on unsteady legs and sat on the sofa. She stared at me a moment, and there were tears in her eyes.

"You're not human."

I shrugged. "Maybe. I do what it takes to survive. Being sentimental and emotional is a problem for survival. Sometimes loyalty and fidelity will get you killed. So I do what I have to do, and I survive. I'm good at that."

"Is it worth it?" She asked the question staring at the carpet. Then she raised her eyes to meet mine. "Living with no loyalty? Living for the sake of living, without love or commitment or..."

She trailed off, and I said, "Subjugation?"

Her frown deepened. "Subjugation? Is that how you think of it?"

"When one person controls another, owns them, makes them do what he wants them to do, that is subjugation. It was what Gabbai and Del wanted to do with me. They wanted to own me, control me, subjugate me. That's what their faith is all about. It's what Islam means: subjugation."

"Why are you telling me this?"

"So that you know who I am."

She looked away, then down at her glass. "I know who you are."

I took a pull on my whiskey. As I set the glass down, I said, "I'll make the transfer. Then you can leave and start to rebuild your life."

"That's it? You put me through all this, you take me to hell and back, you murder everybody in sight, and then you just pay me off and send me away? That's it? That's your solution?"

"No!" I snarled it at her. "It's not my solution. It's not anybody's solution. There are no solutions, Chelsea. Life's a bitch and then you die. You make your choices and you take the consequences. I warned you not to get involved. I warned you not to bring the kids along. But you insisted you wanted to do it and you wanted to come along. So this is where your damn choices have brought you. You've got ten million bucks in Belize. So get a damn therapist!"

I turned, making for the stairs to go get my laptop. I heard her get to her feet behind me.

"Harry, wait."

I turned back. "What?"

"Don't."

"What are you talking about? Don't what? You're telling me you don't want ten million bucks and a house in Belize?"

"Please stop being like this, Harry. It's not you. I know it's not really you. Doesn't any of what we've been through mean anything to you?"

"We talked about this."

"You talked. I just had to sit and listen."

I ran my fingers through my hair. "What do you want, Chelsea? You want us to get married? You want the house with the white picket fence? I can't do that. I can't be that. What will we have in our photo albums? Pictures of my beheaded best friend? Who's going to be the best man at our wedding, the Kiwi?"

She covered her face and started weeping. She got to her feet and came over to me, put her arms around my waist, and buried her face in my chest. She kept repeating, over and over, "Please stop. Please, please just stop!" She took my face in her hands. Her eyes were swollen and wet, like her lips. "Harry, please, take me upstairs."

"'I can't do this."

"Please, Harry, I'm cracking up. It's been too much. Too much killing. Too much suffering. Please! I need you to hold me. Just hold me and tell me it's going to be OK. Please!"

I practically carried her up the stairs. Her legs were giving way every couple of steps, and her crying had become convulsive, almost as though she was retching. I didn't bother removing her clothes. I took off her shoes and eased her under the covers. Then I took off my boots and got in beside her and held her. We lay like that for maybe fifteen minutes until her breathing had slowed and steadied and I was sure she was asleep. Then I eased out of bed, careful not to wake her, and put three cushions where my body had been. Then I went and sat in the chair by the window and played over everything that had happened since Sheriff Seth Levi had called me in Pinedale. I went over it in minute detail, right up to the point where I had shot the brigadier and the president's personal advisors, and then blown Del all the way up to his seventy-two virgins. If they could put him together again, they were welcome to him.

After an hour, her breathing changed. First it stopped. Then it became deeper but slower. There was movement in the bed, slow at first and then quick and explosive with a savage scream as she started pounding the cushions.

I reached over and flipped on the light. She froze, staring at me. She said, "What the...?" Then, "My God! I had a nightmare. They were trying to kill me. I was fighting for my life..."

I jerked my chin at her hand. "Is that where you got the knife? From the nightmare?"

"No! No, Harry, ever since all this happened and Dave was killed, I've been carrying this knife. You can't think— Thank God you'd gotten up! Oh, Harry! To think I might have hurt you!"

She swung her legs out of bed and sat staring at me.

"Dave," I said. "You'd known him a while, right? Long enough to make contact professionally, negotiate a deal, go through pre-production, start production. I'm no expert, but I'd say we're talking at least a year, right?"

She'd gone very quiet. "What are you getting at?" It was almost a whisper.

"You didn't cry when he died. You were more interested in negotiating with me to rescue the show."

"I told you at the time, I have trouble expressing my emotions. Harry, you can't think—"

"Yeah, you had the same trouble when Dyno was killed, and Paul."

"Harry, I don't know what the hell you're getting at, but I really don't need this right now."

"But you know what I thought was really interesting? When that emotional barrier came down. It came down when I killed Gabbai. Then you began to go to pieces."

"For Christ's sake, Harry! I killed a man to save your life!"

"Or to silence him."

"This is insane! I have been the *victim* in all this! I have stood with you every inch of the way! Do you think, do you think just maybe, I broke down when you killed *all* those men, as well as Gabbai, there might have been a *cumulative* effect at work there? Is that just *fucking* possible? I don't know how many violent murders you can handle one after another, Harry, but I had reached my *limit!*"

"That's what I told myself. But then, through the whole business with Gabbai, when I offered to join him, you never —not once—suggested going to the Feds. You never told me you couldn't be a part of it. You never tried to get away or contact your friends in LA to ask for help."

"I trusted you," she said simply.

"You know what, Chelsea? That is probably the stupidest thing you have said since I met you. And you have said some pretty stupid things. You trusted a man who was prepared to sell out to his sworn enemy and murder and behead his commanding officer?"

"But you said you would never let any harm come to me. You said that! That was the very reason you were going to kill the brigadier and those other men, to save me!"

I gave my head a small shake and gave a small laugh. "And that didn't strike you as odd?"

Her jaw actually dropped. "Oh," she said. "Oh my God."

I smiled. "You were just *too* keen to have those kids follow us. And there could be only one reason for that. When we got the boat at Long Lake, at the foot of Sacred Rim, you were not crying from trauma or relief. I have seen that kind of crying many times. You were crying from grief, at having lost Gabbai."

"What reason would I have for encouraging those kids to follow us? Show me! Show me the depth of your paranoia!"

"It was Del and Gabbai's revenge, their way of punishing me. They knew that death was not a big deal for me. So killing me would not satisfy. They knew, since Al-Landy, that what really hurt me was killing innocent, vulnerable people in my care. You knew that, and that's why you encouraged them to come along. There is no other explanation for such a stupid, irresponsible act.

"I'll tell you something else. When I climbed in the SUV this evening, you were not scared. You were sulking. And at no time did Del or Gabbai show hostility to you—"

"You mean except when he had that ape point a gun at my head!"

"I have seen those men, and their uncle, beat, whip, maim, and murder women at the slightest provocation—or with no provocation at all. He never came close to ordering you harmed in the slightest way."

"Because he knew if he did he would lose his power over you!"

"And tell me something, Chelsea. What could have given him that idea? Where did he get that notion if he had never seen us together until then?"

She sat staring at me for a long time. Finally she said, in a very small voice, "I don't know. Maybe he saw something in your eyes."

"Yeah, maybe, or maybe you phoned him after we hit the sack and told him you had seduced me, and I was vulnerable."

"Harry, that isn't true. For God's sake!"

"When that plane exploded on the runway, you went into shock. You were not relieved to be free of the man who was threatening to destroy your life. You were gutted, devastated, that your whole organization had just been wiped out. Tell me something. Did you love Gabbai and Del? Were they family to you? More than that? When did they recruit you? From college?"

Her voice was barely a whisper. "Please, Harry. You have to stop this. You are slipping into a paranoid fantasy. Please stop."

"Who recruited the ninja who killed Dave?" She stared at me, but she didn't answer. "I got the brigadier to find out. It was you. You didn't go to a talent agent. He was a friend of yours. You had him show up for an audition, and you recruited him. As the producer, you could do that."

I paused. She still didn't say anything.

"What about Ernie?" I said. "Did you recruit his killer too? Or did Gabbai take care of that?"

"Harry, you have to stop this. You are just grabbing at random, unrelated facts and stitching together a patchwork quilt of evidence that looks convincing until you stop to analyze it. Rashid—that was the ninja—he was a young guy who'd been hanging around the studio, making friends with people, boasting about his martial arts skills. We all discussed it, and we all decided he was a good fit. It wasn't *me* specifically who employed him."

She stood. "Please, Harry. We have been good together. I know you have feelings for me, and for some crazy reason, in spite of all this craziness, I have feelings for you too. You must know, looking at me, knowing me like you do, that I am incapable of hurting a fly! Please, Harry, can we put this behind us and just"—she shook her head and laughed—"take the money and run! Let's *go* to Belize, start a new life, learn to trust and love each other. I *know* I can make you happy! And I know that if you will just drop this, maybe seek some kind of therapy, I know you can learn to love me. Just let go, Harry, and let's do it."

She took a couple of faltering steps until she stood right in front of me. She held out her hands. The knife was gone. Her eyes were red from crying, and her lips were swollen with grief. I took her hands and stood, and she embraced me with her arms squeezing tightly around my waist and her head on my shoulder, soaking my shirt with her tears.

TWENTY

I took her face in my hands, feeling the wetness of her cheeks. "There is something you need to know," I said.

She shook her head, looking up into my face, crying convulsively. "I don't want to. I don't want to know anything else. I just want us to go away."

"What did they promise you, Chelsea? What did they promise you if you joined them?" She was still shaking her head. "Was it wealth? Was it power? Or was it forgiveness? A guaranteed place in heaven, beside a god who would forgive everything, provided you subjugated yourself to him? What was it?"

"I don't care, Harry. It doesn't matter. You're wrong. I never did any of it. Please, just stop and let's go away."

"We don't need to go away."

She screwed up her face. "What?"

"We don't need to go away. They are all dead. Gabbai, Del, Mohammed Ben-Amini, all of them are dead."

She gave her head a small, tight shake and wiped her eyes with her fingers and her nose with the back of her wrist. "But the Feds, the Secret Service..."

"We don't need to worry about them, Chelsea. We don't need to run away anywhere." I stroked her cheeks, looking into her eyes, trying to read what was hidden in them. "What did they promise you, Chelsea? They promised me your life, your servitude, you as my woman. I didn't want it. I lied to them to gain their trust. Because I knew from the start that I was going to kill them for what they had done in Al-Landy. What did they promise you?"

"You didn't want me?"

"I wanted you if you were for real. I'd have wanted you if it came from you. But I don't want any woman who comes as a gift from another man or a god. She comes of her own will, or she doesn't come at all. What did they promise you, Chelsea?"

"There is no way I can ever make you believe me, is there?"

"I told you there was something you needed to know. There was fifty pounds of C4 in that bomb that killed Del." She stared at me and swallowed. The crying had stopped. "That much C4 would not fit in that carton with four heads."

"But he looked in the carton. I looked in the carton. The heads were there."

"They were made of Latex and packed with plastic explosive."

She took a step back. Her eyes were wide. Her jaw sagged. It was the same expression I had seen on her face when the jet exploded. She shook her head. "You shot them."

"How do you know?"

"You *shot them!*"

"*How do you know?*"

"*Because I heard you! The guy in the car recorded it! You shot them!*"

"We knew you'd be listening in at the very least, possibly recording it for distribution to the media. So we set it up. The whole thing. Down to the pigs' blood in the carton, the shock and horror of the victims. Everything."

"So the brigadier, General Moorcroft, General Schwarz, and Admiral Sam Benner, they are all still alive..."

"Yes. I told you. We don't have to escape anywhere."

She smiled. Then she started laughing and wiping her eyes. "But Harry, that's wonderful! We are safe! We are in the clear! Everything is *fine!*"

The last word came out as a scream as she lunged at me with the knife suddenly in her right hand. I grabbed her wrist out of pure reflex, but she slashed at the back of my hand with the blade. I let go and stepped back, reaching for the Sig in my waistband, but I knew I wouldn't have time. She was going to stab me and kill me. There was nothing I could do about it, and I felt a certain peace. The fighting, the struggling, the killing, and the pain were finally over.

The report filled the whole world with the explosion, and she stopped dead in her tracks. There was a red hole the size of a penny in her left chest, but a lot of blood had sprayed out of her back, over the bed. She went down on her knees, and I moved to her, beside her. She looked up into my face. Her eyes were confused and sad. When she spoke, it was barely a whisper. "They promised me God," she said. "And forgiveness."

Her eyes went out, like they'd cut the supply. I stood and turned to the door. The Kiwi was there, fishing a Camel from his soft pack.

"Sorry," he said. "I know you cared about her."

He poked the cigarette in his mouth and leaned into the flame of his lighter.

"Yeah. I knew what she was, but I had hoped."

"Will you call Buddy or should I?"

I pulled my cell from my pocket and dialed the number.

"Harry." For the first time in the years I'd known him, he sounded worried. "Everything OK?"

"Yeah," I said, and sighed. "Everybody's dead."

Don't miss THE CELL. The riveting sequel in the Harry Bauer Thriller series.

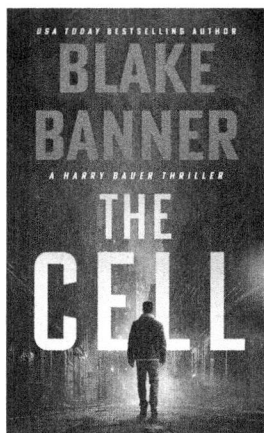

Scan the QR code below to purchase THE CELL.

Or go to: righthouse.com/the-cell

NOTE: flip to the very end to read an exclusive sneak peak...

DON'T MISS ANYTHING!

If you want to stay up to date on all new releases in this series, with this author, or with any of our new deals, you can do so by joining our newsletters below.

In addition, you will immediately gain access to our entire *Right House VIP Library,* which includes many riveting Mystery and Thriller novels for your enjoyment!

righthouse.com/email

(Easy to unsubscribe. No spam. Ever.)

ALSO BY BLAKE BANNER

Up to date books can be found at:
www.righthouse.com/blake-banner

ROGUE THRILLERS
Gates of Hell (Book 1)
Hell's Fury (Book 2)
Ice Burn (Book 3)

ALEX MASON THRILLERS
Odin (Book 1)
Ice Cold Spy (Book 2)
Mason's Law (Book 3)
Assets and Liabilities (Book 4)
Russian Roulette (Book 5)
Executive Order (Book 6)
Dead Man Talking (Book 7)
All The King's Men (Book 8)
Flashpoint (Book 9)
Brotherhood of the Goat (Book 10)
Dead Hot (Book 11)
Blood on Megiddo (Book 12)
Son of Hell (Book 13)
Merchant of Death (Book 14)

HARRY BAUER THRILLER SERIES
Dead of Night (Book 1)
Dying Breath (Book 2)

The Einstaat Brief (Book 3)
Quantum Kill (Book 4)
Immortal Hate (Book 5)
The Silent Blade (Book 6)
LA: Wild Justice (Book 7)
Breath of Hell (Book 8)
Invisible Evil (Book 9)
The Shadow of Ukupacha (Book 10)
Sweet Razor Cut (Book 11)
Blood of the Innocent (Book 12)
Blood on Balthazar (Book 13)
Simple Kill (Book 14)
Riding The Devil (Book 15)
The Unavenged (Book 16)
The Devil's Vengeance (Book 17)
Bloody Retribution (Book 18)
Rogue Kill (Book 19)
Blood for Blood (Book 20)
The Cell (Book 21)
Time to Die (Book 22)

DEAD COLD MYSTERY SERIES
An Ace and a Pair (Book 1)
Two Bare Arms (Book 2)
Garden of the Damned (Book 3)
Let Us Prey (Book 4)
The Sins of the Father (Book 5)
Strange and Sinister Path (Book 6)
The Heart to Kill (Book 7)
Unnatural Murder (Book 8)
Fire from Heaven (Book 9)

To Kill Upon A Kiss (Book 10)
Murder Most Scottish (Book 11)
The Butcher of Whitechapel (Book 12)
Little Dead Riding Hood (Book 13)
Trick or Treat (Book 14)
Blood Into Wine (Book 15)
Jack In The Box (Book 16)
The Fall Moon (Book 17)
Blood In Babylon (Book 18)
Death In Dexter (Book 19)
Mustang Sally (Book 20)
A Christmas Killing (Book 21)
Mommy's Little Killer (Book 22)
Bleed Out (Book 23)
Dead and Buried (Book 24)
In Hot Blood (Book 25)
Fallen Angels (Book 26)
Knife Edge (Book 27)
Along Came A Spider (Book 28)
Cold Blood (Book 29)
Curtain Call (Book 30)

THE OMEGA SERIES
Dawn of the Hunter (Book 1)
Double Edged Blade (Book 2)
The Storm (Book 3)
The Hand of War (Book 4)
A Harvest of Blood (Book 5)
To Rule in Hell (Book 6)
Kill: One (Book 7)
Powder Burn (Book 8)

ABOUT US

Right House is an independent publisher created by authors for readers. We specialize in Action, Thriller, Mystery, and Crime novels.

If you enjoyed this novel, then there is a good chance you will like what else we have to offer! Please stay up to date by using any of the links below.

Join our mailing lists to stay up to date -->
righthouse.com/email
Visit our website --> righthouse.com
Contact us --> contact@righthouse.com

facebook.com/righthousebooks
x.com/righthousebooks
instagram.com/righthousebooks

EXCLUSIVE SNEAK PEEK OF...

THE CELL

CHAPTER ONE

I HAVE LIVED HAUNTED BY THE VISION OF A child's eyes.

I am not a religious man. I believe in reality. Maybe there is a greater truth back of that reality, underlying it. I don't know. I don't think anybody does. But one thing I am sure of is that the path to that truth, if it exists, does not involve hating and sentencing to death all those who stray from your idea of what is right.

That child could not have been more than four or five years old. She was pretty with very black hair and dark eyes. She was one of the people massacred at Al-Landy, where, in the name of God, in the name of what was right according to their religion, every man, woman, and child was murdered after being tortured, raped, or both. Their crime had been a crime against God. Their crime was wanting to buy a TV for the village café, and that constituted blasphemy, a denial of God.

I was there with my patrol, hidden in the sand dunes

above the village, and I watched it happen. I watched them through the scope on my C8 Carbine. I watched them drive in in their trucks with their guns. I watched them round up the village. Somehow my eyes had locked on to that little girl's eyes, and her fear and grief was burned into my mind. I never knew her name. I never knew her parents or her family. All I knew was her terror, her pain, and her deep sadness. They became a part of me, a part of what I had become.

A killer.

I don't do therapy. I don't think there are many people in this world who would know how to heal the massacre at Al-Landy. But a few months back, I ran into an old friend, Sam Jorgensen, who had spent several years with Delta Force and had seen his fair share of the darkness human beings are capable of creating. When he retired, he'd devoted his life to studying the human mind and got doctorates in psychology and philosophy. We'd gotten drunk together, and I'd told him about Al-Landy and the fact that I had hunted down the man responsible for the massacre, Mohammed Ben Amini, and I had killed him. But the little girl's eyes still haunted me.

He had told me to bury her. To find a place that was peaceful and quiet, undisturbed by human madness, to take something that represented her and bury it in that place and give her peace. A place where her soul could be at peace.

It took me seven months to build up the courage, but I'd finally decided to get the rifle and the scope through which I had watched the massacre, take them up to the Wind River Mountains in Wyoming, as high as I could climb, to those places where, when you look down, you feel your soul could take off and fly, and there bury that child, give her soul peace and, if there is a God of Love and Forgiveness, commit her soul to that god's care.

I had wrapped my C8 Carbine and scope in black silk and placed them in a wooden box. Then I had climbed into my Grenadier truck outside my old brownstone on James Baldwin Place and driven the two thousand plus miles to Pinedale. It took me all of thirty-four hours because I stopped on the way at a motel for a few hours' sleep.

Once in Pinedale, I stopped again, briefly, at my house on Pole Creek Road. There I showered, had coffee, and grabbed a bottle of whiskey. Then I drove to the Sacred Rim trailhead. From there, I walked for a couple of hours into the mountains, carrying the boxed C8 Carbine and scope on my back, past Photographer's Point to a place where Freemont Creek tumbles out of the Winds into a deep canyon on its journey toward Freemont Lake. The view from there cannot be described with words, but it always seems to me to defy gravity and makes you believe that perhaps, after all, we have a soul, and that soul can rise above the hell that is this world and fly.

It was while I sat there with these rare thoughts, mourning a child I never had, whose name I did not even know, mourning the childhood she might have had, the happiness she might have had, and the existence I myself might have had—devoted to life instead of death—it was while I was mourning that child and preparing to lay her to rest that my phone rang.

There is no signal at that height in the Wind River Mountains. Phones don't work up there. Which meant the call could have come from just one person.

I closed my eyes, swore as one is not supposed to swear at

a funeral, decided firmly not to answer it, and put it to my ear.

"Sir?"

The brigadier's clipped English voice answered. "Harry, are you in New York?"

"No."

"How soon can you get back? It's urgent."

I sighed quietly. "I'll leave my truck here and get a plane. Give me maybe six or seven hours."

There was a frown in his voice. "Where are you?"

I hesitated a fraction of a second. "Pinedale."

"Oh. Claire?"

"No. I'm up in the mountains."

"I see. I'm sorry to interrupt. It's important. You'll see when you get here. What's your nearest airport? Ralph Wenz, isn't it?"

"Yeah."

"That's a little less than two thousand miles. I'll send the company plane. Give him three or four hours. I'll call you when he's about to touch down."

"You're sending the plane? It's that important?"

"Yes. That important."

"OK, I'm on my way."

I said it without enthusiasm, hung up, sighed deeply, and looked up into the vast blue dome of the sky. I spoke across time to someplace outside of space where I wanted to believe she could hear me.

"I'll come back," I said. "I'll set you free." And as I spoke, a name came to me. A name that made me smile. I shrugged, and after a moment I added, "Miriam." She'd looked like a Miriam, I decided.

I made my way back through the pinewoods to the trail-head. There I packed the stuff carefully in the truck, and on the drive back to my house on Pole Creek Road, as the sun blazed across the western horizon, I wondered what was so important that the brigadier would send Cobra's specially adapted long haul Gulfstream to get me back to New York in the shortest time modern technology would allow. Israel, Iran, Syria, Ukraine, and North Korea all passed through my mind, but they were not my department. There were other agencies that took care of international crises of that sort. I was strictly a hit man—and a semi-retired one at that. I'd be fully retired, I told myself as I pulled up outside my house, if they'd let me.

———

I SLEPT through the flight and touched down in Teterboro just after midnight. There was a Grand Cherokee waiting for me with a driver in a blue suit who might have been an android with limited artificial intelli-gence. He asked me if I was me, and when I told him I was, he carried my bag to the Jeep and drove me, through the sleeping darkness of suburban street lamps, to the Cobra headquarters one and a half miles north of Pleas-antville.

There, after going through the elaborate security of facial recognition and voice recognition, I was led across a checkerboard floor to the library, where I found the brigadier seated in his chesterfield in front of the fire. He stood as I was shown in and approached me with both hands outstretched.

"Harry, good of you to come at such short notice. Have you eaten? Will you have a drink?"

I told him I was fine, but he ignored me and poured us a whiskey each anyway. He sat as he handed me my drink and sighed.

"This is a unique situation, Harry. I am aware you are in need of time to think about your future and whether you want to continue as an operative with Cobra or not, and I would not, under any other circumstances, have troubled you."

I sipped my drink and set it down on the table beside me.

"You don't normally talk around a subject either, sir. I'm here. What's it about?"

He took another deep breath. "Cobra is not officially sanctioned, as you know. However, within that, we operate under tight rules, and we are very careful about how we select our targets, and we have very strict criteria."

"Crimes against humanity."

"Quite, and that is strictly defined. As you know, we are very careful to avoid a culture of just picking off anyone who gets on some Western leader's nerves. The risk is there and constant, and we guard against it."

I nodded, smiled, and spread my hands. "So...?"

"There is an exception to every rule, and that exception has cropped up with a vengeance, if you will forgive the expression."

I arched an eyebrow at him. "An exception? What kind of an exception?"

"Before I tell you, let me just say this. You will be briefed, and if you decide you don't want to do the job, you will be flown back to Pinedale, or wherever you want to go, and the case will be closed and shelved. You understand that? You are the only operative I know of to whom I would entrust this job."

"I'm flattered. What is the job?"

"You have heard of Jeff Cook."

It wasn't a question, but I said, "Yes, of course. The founder of the Clearwater Corporation. He's a tech giant, defense contractor..." I frowned, unaware of his involvement in any kind of crime against humanity. "Is he the target?"

"No. I am not sure if you are aware of it, but his wife was killed in a traffic accident a couple of years ago. They had one daughter, Beverly. She was twelve at the time of her mother's death. She and her father live together at Clearlake, about an hour's drive north of San Francisco. As you can imagine, after the mother's death, she and her father became very close. She is home schooled..." He trailed off, making circular 'on and on' motions with his hand that somehow suggested she and her dad hung out together a lot. I hazarded a guess.

"Jeff Cook is a friend of yours."

"Yes. We have been friends for some time."

He watched me. I drew breath and picked up my drink. "You said this is a job you would only entrust to me, and you've made a point of mentioning his daughter. She is what, fourteen now?"

"Yes."

"I am guessing this involves the child, and that is why you want me to do the job."

"She has been abducted."

"Do we know who by?"

The brigadier gave a kind of wince. "Yes and no. Jeff received a video which I'll show you later. The man who sent it calls himself Hussein-i Sabbah."

"Wasn't that the name of the Persian head of the Hashishim?"

"Hassan-i Sabbah, founder of the Nizari Ismai'li sect, otherwise known as the Hashishim. Precisely. And you are quite right; Hussein is the diminutive of Hassan. The thing is, we have no record of this man. Neither have Central Intelligence or the Federal Bureau of Investigation. I have spoken to ODIN—"

"Odin? The Norse god?" I smiled. "I didn't realize you were so well connected, sir."

He narrowed his eyes, and his mouth twitched like he wasn't sure whether to laugh or not. "They are unofficial, like us. They don't really exist, but they manage and coordinate the flow of intelligence from the Five Eyes."

"I thought the NSA did that."

"They wish. However, the point is ODIN hasn't heard of him either."

"So he's a rogue operator."

"That was the initial view, but there are indications he may have wider and deeper connections. He makes reference to things that only a well-connected operator would have knowledge of."

"Like?"

"Training camps and bases in Iran, events in East Africa no one would know about unless they were well connected. I'll acquaint you with all of this in a moment. But first let me make this clear: Cobra cannot employ you to find this girl. That is not our brief. We are exclusively concerned with eliminating a particular class of international criminal, as you know. On the other hand, we don't have the kind of information that would allow us to classify this Hussein-i Sabbah as one of that class of criminal—as having committed crimes against humanity, and thus have a justi-fied reason to send you after him."

I frowned. "So what am I doing here?"

He smiled. "You are not here. You are up in the Wind River Mountains. What I have suggested to Jeff is that he employ you, privately, to recover his daughter—"

I interrupted him. "Sir, I am a soldier, not a detective. That is a job for the feds. They have the skills and the resources."

He shook his head. "In the first place, between us, Cobra and the Clearwater Corporation have technological resources that the FBI can only dream about. In the second place, working directly for Jeff, you have unlimited access to a hundred billion dollars in financial resources. In addition to that, he cannot *brief* the Bureau. He cannot give them a task—a mission—and tell them how he wants it done. If he reported it to the Bureau, their protocols would kick in, and the machine would take over. As a result, they would investi-gate, Beverly would get killed, or worse, and Hussein would disappear. But if he briefs *you*, secretly, with no press coverage or leaky officials involved, they will not be expecting you. And you will have a very precise brief, a brief the FBI could never have: Bring Beverly safely home and kill Hussein-i Sabbah."

CHAPTER TWO

HE REACHED DOWN TO THE TABLE BY HIS SIDE AND pressed a remote control. The lights dimmed, and a TV screen emerged from the cabinet against the wall. It remained black for a moment. Then suddenly there was a young girl. She was about fourteen or fifteen but still child-like. Her face showed she was terrified, her cheeks glistened with tears, her eyes were puffy and red, and her mouth was pulled down in an expression of grief and fear. I felt a hot coal of rage in my belly.

A man appeared from off-screen and sat next to her. He was in a white robe and had a white turban wound around his head, but his face was obscured by a black scarf. Behind them, there was a window, but it had been smeared over with black paint, and only a couple of glimmers of light shone through at the edges. There were faint, dim noises which were hard to distinguish. The girl's sobbing was clearly audible. The man spoke suddenly. His voice was slightly muffled by the scarf.

"Good morning, Mr. Cook. How does it feel to be the richest man in the world today?" He had a very slight accent, but his English was that of a man who had been through an elite English education—Eton or Harrow and then Oxford. "How does the value of all that wealth stack up against the loss of your daughter? Do you feel rich and privileged right now?"

He stopped talking and looked down at the floor.

"I'll tell you what I think, Mr. Cook. I think that right now"—he raised his head to look at the camera again—"you are the poorest man on the planet. Because you have lost the only truly valuable thing you had, and your world is now a world of pain." He shook his head. "It does not get any better. It only gets worse and more painful. I will tell you what comes next. I will marry your daughter, and she will become my possession, my chattel. We will live together in Sartakht. I will beat her often to keep her in submission. She will bear me children, and she will raise them to be great warriors and heroes. You will see them born, and you will see their birthdays. You will see them graduate to Rafsanjan, and you will see your daughter raise them, like the cow, like the breeding beast that she is. And one day, Mr. Cook, your daughter will be raped by my men. I will accuse her of adultery, and she will be executed, buried up to her neck in sand, and stoned to death. I will film the whole thing for you so that you can have a record of your daughter's useful life and death."

He spread his hands. "Can you stop this from happening? Of course. Obedience and subjugation will always bring God's favor. But I do not have to tell you exactly what to do. Your own conscience will guide you. We will talk, Mr. Cook.

You can crawl to me on your knees, and you can tell me what steps you have taken to bring God's favor upon you."

He turned to Beverly. "You want to say some words to your father?"

She nodded and spoke through her sobs. "I love you, Daddy, and tell Aunt Bella Aurora I love her and miss her. And please, follow the path of subjugation to God."

Hussein leaned forward toward the camera, and it went black. The lights came up. I said, "Who is Aunt Bella Aurora?"

"We have no idea, and Jeff has no idea either. We are trying to work it out."

"What about the noises and the patches of light through the pane on the window?"

"We have forensic specialists working on both, but so far, we have very little to go on."

I nodded. Something was nagging at the back of my mind. While I let the back of my mind work at it, I said, "Sartakht and Rafsanjan, what are these places?"

He gave a single nod and took a pull on his drink. As he set it down, he said, "It's what I mentioned to you earlier. There are very few people that know about either of those places. The fact that he knows about both says a lot. Sartakht is a training camp deep in the Zagros mountain range. It specializes in very particular kinds of terrorism, from cyber terrorism to mental conditioning and esoteric stuff like that. Rafsanjan is a research center, part of a network that specializes in weapons of mass destruction. Both have close ties with a number of terrorist organizations. Not just jihadist ones, either. They are working increasingly closely with Russia and North Korea."

"So where do I start?"

"You'll do it?"

"Of course. But I'm not real clear yet what *it* is. How did the abduction happen? Were there any witnesses? Do we have any forensics, fingerprints, DNA...?" He drew breath to answer, but I interrupted him. "Why is Cook not here to tell me himself?"

He shook his head. "There can be no personal contact between you and Cook. He must have absolute deniability, not just plausible but indisputable. Besides, I can take you through the whole thing, probably better than he can."

"You were there?" I tried to keep the irony out of my voice but didn't do a great job.

"No, and neither was he. But where he is emotionally distraught, I am not. So I can be more objective. Shall I walk you through what we know?"

"Yeah."

He pulled an old-fashioned rope hanging from the ceiling beside his chair, and a moment later, a man in a white jacket with white gloves stepped in. The brigadier said, "We'll need some sandwiches—cheese, ham, pickles, you know the sort of thing."

The man muttered that he knew and withdrew. The brigadier sipped his whisky, and as he set down his glass, he said, "I mentioned that Beverly was home schooled. She had a number of tutors for specific subjects, but then there was one tutor who gave her a solid grounding in general knowledge—a basic educational foundation, as it were."

"His name?"

"Oliver Brown. He appeared to have good references, which were followed up—"

220 | BLAKE BANNER

"How long ago was that?"

"Two years ago last July, shortly after Adriana's death."

"Adriana was the mother?"

"Yes. Oliver spent August preparing the curriculum, and they started their lessons toward the end of September. They were apparently fond of him. He was by all accounts a good teacher. Beverly liked him, and he never showed any signs of eccentricity, religious fanaticism, or anything peculiar of that nature."

There was a knock at the door, and a pretty maid in uniform came in and placed two plates of sandwiches on a table between us. She gave me a smile and withdrew. I picked up a ham sandwich and said, "From the way you're talking, you think he took the girl."

He kind of winced. "The fact is voice recognition software has him as *probably* the man on the video. In terms of build, he is roughly the same. Oliver had a normal West Coast accent. The man in the video has more of a Middle Eastern accent, but an accent is the easiest thing in the world to imitate."

I was frowning as I chewed. I watched him reach for a cheese sandwich. "Sir, voice recognition is pretty compelling evidence. Add to that the fact that he was familiar with the family's movements and with Beverly's timetable, and it's a pretty strong case. Yet I can see you have doubts."

"You're absolutely right." He said it around a chunk of sandwich he was chewing. "Everything points to him. My only reservation is that I know Oliver, and I am a pretty good judge of men, and I just don't see Oliver doing something like this. It takes a lot of grit to plan and, above all, execute an operation of this sort. Oliver just didn't strike me as the type." He raised his shoulders an eighth of an inch. "But again, all that means is that I may not be as sharp as I believe I am. Or that Oliver, like many sociopaths, is an extremely good liar."

I grunted and sipped my whiskey. "So what happened?"

He picked up his glass and sat back. "Four days ago—" He paused to look at his watch. "Yes, almost exactly four days ago, Jeff took his car and drove down to San Jose. That's where Clearwater has its head office. It was what he did every Monday, Wednesday, and Friday. The rest of the time he worked from home. When he was at the office, he left his daughter in the care of her tutor—"

"Oliver Brown."

"Correct—Angelita, the nanny, and Mrs. Noaks, the cook. Part of the day, there was also a cleaner. She came in from nine until four, then went home. Jeff would have left the office at four, and by then, Beverly would have been in the care of Mrs. Noaks."

"What time did Cook come home?"

"It's a three-hour drive from San Jose. He left the office at four to beat the rush hour and arrived home at just after seven."

"By which time, Beverly would have been alone with her nanny and the cook for two and a half hours."

The brigadier nodded. "Yes, only she wasn't there. The front door was open, Angelita's car was there, but there was no sign of Angelita, Mrs. Noaks, or Beverly. Jeff called to them but got no response—until he went into the kitchen."

There was a horrible inevitability about it. I said, "He found them there dead."

"They had both, Angelita and Mrs. Noaks, been shot in

the head. A single shot. Mrs. Noaks in the left temple, where she was sitting at the kitchen table, and Angelita between the eyes, as though she had turned from what she was doing at the sink."

"So he is unemotional and well-trained. Probably a professional."

"It certainly looks that way."

"Does that sound like the tutor, Oliver Brown?"

"No, not in the least."

"And Cook's first reaction was to call you?"

"It was clear Beverly had been abducted, and he knew that I could get her back more quickly and more efficiently than a state bureaucracy."

I frowned. "How come he knows about Cobra?"

"He doesn't, though as a major defense contractor, he has top security clearance. Besides which, he knows that I am involved in black ops for the US and the UK. So we got a couple teams in to go over the house, and we got exactly nothing. There were the fingerprints you would expect to get, and aside from that, only negatives. The house had not been broken into, there were no boot prints, powder burns, stray hairs, bits of cotton—nothing. A minor consolation was that there were no traces of blood either, other than those from Mrs. Noaks and Angelita."

"So we can say that the abduction took place some time between four p.m. when the cleaner left and seven when Cook got home."

"Yes, that's how I see it."

"What about the cleaner?"

"A retired village woman, three generations in the

town, absolutely no connections with crime or terrorism. We have screened her and questioned her. She's in the clear."

"What about the cops?"

"They have been instructed to stand down, it's being taken care of at a higher level."

"So the only person unaccounted for is Oliver Brown, the tutor, and voice recognition places him as the guy in the video."

The brigadier nodded. "Not one hundred percent, but very probably."

"What do you know about his background?"

"Native of Napa, sixty miles down the hill, younger brother, older sister, middle-class family, comfortably well off, did well at school, Methodist but not practicing, degree from UCLA in psychology, trained as a teacher. No record of any kind. Generally unremarkable."

"Obviously you've checked his online presence."

"Facebook, X, Reddit, LinkedIn, and we checked his messaging services and telephone records. Either he was working solo or, as is increasingly the case these days, he was using conventional craft, dead drops, physical meetings face to face, coded classified ads..."

"Cold war stuff."

"Effective and very hard to trace."

I pointed at the black TV screen. "I want to watch that again a few times tonight. Can you make it available in my room?"

"Of course."

"And send it to my phone."

"Sure. I'll send you a photograph of Oliver too."

"And I want to go and see Oliver's parents and Cook's house."

"That's arranged already. We fly in..." He looked at his watch. "Six hours."

I made to stand. "I'm going to get some sleep. Am I in the same room?"

"Your room, yes."

"Is there anything else I need to know?"

He gave his head a single shake. "You have the basics. You understand, whoever did this, we don't want them alive."

"I know." I stood and hesitated. "Is there any chance Oliver was taken too?"

He smiled. "I know. It's the first thing that comes to mind. But it seems to be him in that video. The simplest explanation, Harry, is that we are looking at a dissociative personality disorder."

"A split personality?"

He mixed a shrug with a nod. "It's more like two distinct personalities inhabiting one mind. But right now, the evidence points to the fact that Oliver Brown has abducted Beverly Cook. And if that is the case, then we hunt him down, and we kill him."

I nodded, left him sitting by the fire, and made my way up the old mahogany stairs to my room. There I sat on the end of the bed and played the video over several times until all I could hear in my head was the fear in Beverly's voice as she sobbed out, "I love you, Daddy, and tell Aunt Bella Aurora I love her and miss her. And please, follow the path of subjugation to God."

"*...tell Aunt Bella Aurora I love her...*"

I went and showered, hot then cold, then hot and cold again and came back to the bed drying my hair. I put the video on again, over and over, and the more I listened to it, the more I filtered out his voice and her voice and focused on the sounds, faint and distant, that came through the painted glass. As I did so, it became more and more obvious that if they had painted the glass, it was because whatever was out there was recognizable. And if that was true, whatever sounds were out there would be recognizable too.

"...*Bella Aurora...*"

Her voice echoed in my mind. Her voice, sobbing in the desert, staring at me, pleading at me with her huge, dark eyes as Mohammed Ben-Amini, the Butcher of Al-Landy, murdered and raped her village, and she cried out, "...*tell Aunt Bella Aurora I love her...*" while the great steam pistons thudded and groaned in the background and I sank into an agony of darkness.

I sat up with a fierce jolt in my heart and reached for the phone.

"Harry? Is everything OK?"

"Yeah. Sorry to wake you, sir. I need the tech guys to isolate those background noises."

"They are barely audible."

"I don't care. Get them to do the best they can. As soon as possible."

"I'll tell them. Get some sleep. We fly in three hours."

I hung up, fell back, and sank into deep sleep.

Scan the QR code below to purchase THE CELL.
Or go to: righthouse.com/the-cell

Printed in Dunstable, United Kingdom